SHERLOCK HOLMES AND THE ADVENTURE OF THE PECULIAR PROVENANCE

Derrick Belanger

© Derrick Belanger 2015.

ISBN-13: 978-1519511959
ISBN-10: 1519511957

Derrick Belanger has asserted his rights under the Copyright, Design and Patents Act, 1988, to be identified as the author of this work.

First ebook published in 2015 by Endeavour Press Ltd. First print edition published in 2015 by Belanger Books, LLC

Dedication

To my father, Dennis Belanger, a lover of all things containing murder and espionage. Dad, I know you would have loved this one!

And

To my brother, Brian Belanger, for always encouraging my writing and forcing me to never give up.

SHERLOCK HOLMES AND THE ADVENTURE OF THE PECULIAR PROVENANCE

Derrick Belanger

Belanger Books

Statements of Advance Praise for *The Adventure of the Peculiar Provenance*

"Derrick Belanger's Sherlock Holmes novella, "The Adventure of the Peculiar Provenance," is a Holmes story written in the grandest tradition of the original Holmes cannon. Technically, the story is written so brilliantly I had to constantly remind myself that Sir Author Conan Doyle himself didn't write it."

- **GC Rosenquist, author of *Sherlock Holmes: The Pearl of Death and Other Early Stories***

"Fantastic tale in classic canonical style - clever (of course, it's Sherlock), action-packed (poor Watson!) with an excellent plot (served with delicious dose of hidden sinister elements) and a well-placed cameo appearance by my personal favourite: The British Government! Holmes and Watson are recognisably themselves, as they always are in the best of pastiches!"

- **Jayantika Ganguly, General Secretary and Editor, Sherlock Holmes Society of India**

"This author truly captures the storytelling virtues with which Doyle imbued Dr. Watson. Belanger's tale pulls you in from the first paragraph, and keeps you at Holmes's side as this marvelous new tale unfolds step-by-step. If you love Holmes, you'll love *The Adventure of the Peculiar Provenance*."

- Kim Krisco, author of *Sherlock Holmes: The Golden Years*

"With *The Adventure of the Peculiar Provenance*, Derrick Belanger has once again created his own unique doorway into the world of Holmes and Watson. He makes you feel as if you're in Victorian London, and the story's twists are both surprising and satisfying."

- David Marcum, author of *The Papers of Sherlock Holmes*

"Once again, Derrick Belanger has captured the flavor and the texture of the Holmesian canon with his best work to date. No Sherlock Holmes fan will be disappointed in this latest work from one of Arthur Conan Doyle's biggest fans."

- C. Edward Davis, author of the Sherlock Holmes story, "The Adventure of the White Bird," in *The MX Book of New Sherlock Holmes stories Part III: 1896 – 1929*

Table of Contents

The Adventure of the Peculiar Provenance ... 9

The Case of the Vanished Killer 117

Author Interview with Derrick Belanger ... 150

The Adventure of the Peculiar Provenance

I had to ask myself, could this be a case that would be too much even for the mind of Sherlock Holmes?

Foreword

It is an honour to bring you the first in a series of adventures based on the newly discovered letters between Dr John H Watson and his nephew Archibald Adams. Archibald is the nephew of Watson's first wife, Constance Adams. He and his uncle had a correspondence that lasted from Archibald's childhood growing up in San Francisco into his adulthood when he resided in Denver, Colorado.

I have known the Adams family for many years and have been their tutor while the children, Michael and Jeanne, have been on summer vacation. I was surprised last summer when I mentioned to Mrs Adams that I was an author who wrote in the style of Dr John Watson.

"Why, Mr Belanger, did you know that I have a connection to Dr Watson? He was a dear friend of my Great-Great-Great Grandfather Archibald Adams." I thought Mrs Adams had made some kind of mistake, but she disappeared to the attic while I continued assisting her children in their lessons. When she returned, she had an old tin box in her hand. "Please, look inside."

I was shocked to discover that the box contained letters from Dr Watson to Archibald Adams. The letters showed a deep friendship between the two men which lasted from Archibald's childhood until the time of Dr Watson's passing. As I read the letters over, I also began to discover that they contained as yet untold stories of that great detective, Mr Sherlock Holmes of 221B Baker St.

With the permission of the Adams family, I have begun to go through the letters and turn these untold tales into narratives written from the point of view of Dr Watson. The case before you, *The Adventure of the Peculiar Provenance*, is the first in what I hope to be many new adventures of the world's first consulting detective, Sherlock Holmes.

I hope you enjoy it!

Sincerely,

Derrick Belanger

THE ADVENTURE OF THE PECULIAR PROVENANCE

Chapter 1

As I have penned many adventures of the heroic feats of my good friend Sherlock Holmes, I have built such a sufficient audience base as to retire fully from my medical practice, and live out the remainder of my years, with my current wife, at our residence on Queen Lucille Street. While the bills of life call for ever more money, and *The Strand* magazine calls for many more of my friend's adventures, occasionally I find Calliope, that strange muse of authors, forcing me to draft stories which will never see the light of day. Such is the case with the adventure contained within these pages. Though I know this story, even now, decades after the events occurred, will never be published as it could negatively impact the economy of Britain, perhaps even the world, and send it spiralling into a great Depression, I still feel the urge to put pen to paper. My coffers may suffer for this, but I cannot help myself, and will tell this story, even if it is to an audience of one.

This adventure begins late in the month of February, 1890. I had been working rather long hours. The month had been a particularly cold, dry one with a bad snowstorm on the fifteenth of February. I had been busy dealing with my patients, a number of whom were suffering from the ailments associated with the frigid weather. Cases of runny noses, fevers, and the more serious pneumonia, had me constantly running between homes and the apothecary from early morning to dusk. The snowstorm on the 15th delayed some of my visits, and I had to spend the following Sunday catching up on seeing my patients. By the time the following weekend approached, I was haggard and weary. My poor Mary, my beautiful wife at the time of this story, who now resides with the angels of Heaven, saw me in such a state, and it caused her great distress.

"My dear, John," she comforted me. "I cannot bear to see you so weak and tired. You must take some time for yourself. You will be no use to your patients if you are on your deathbed, and I fear if you keep working at this pace, you will catch a severe malady yourself, perhaps even consumption."

"You need not worry yourself over me, my precious," I assured her, caressing her pearly cheek. I was afraid my wife's concerns about me, such is the case with the fairer sex, would cause her such distress as to lead to her own set of illnesses. "I am of good health," I continued, "and will have a break from my patients after tomorrow. I have a few house calls to make on Monday morning, and then young Stevens will be on duty for me tomorrow afternoon, and then all of Tuesday and Wednesday."

Relief overtook my wife, and I saw her shoulders relax as she let out a deep sigh. "It will do you good to have some time away. Perhaps," she suggested, "you can see Mr Sherlock Holmes. It always cheers you so to spend time with your dear friend." It had been several weeks since I had seen the great detective, and I agreed it would be nice to pay him a visit.

The next day, between seeing patients and supplying them with their medical needs, I sent a letter to Holmes, and he replied that he would be delighted to dine with me at the

THE ADVENTURE OF THE PECULIAR PROVENANCE

Criterion that evening. After notifying Mary and finishing up another exhausting day, I retired to Piccadilly, and found my friend in the opulent dining room of one of my favourite restaurants.

I wasn't sure if I would see the upbeat version of the detective or the dark and dour man who, without a case to occupy his time, would turn to his pipes and his seven percent solution. Holmes was delighted to see me, and I instantly knew he had not turned to that accursed needle.

"Ah, Watson, so good of you to join me this evening. How is Mary?" he asked. As I chatted with my dear friend over a particularly fine glass of Merlot, I could not help but feel that the detective was distracted, his grey eyes seeming to wander away as I explained about my patients' ailments and the effects of this lingering bitter cold which had enveloped all of London. Clearly, there was something occupying the mind of my dear friend, but he only spoke casually, of Mrs Hudson and his studies of microscopic organisms which can impact a man's health, giving no clue as to the nature of his distraction.

I inquired about my friend's recent cases, and with a wave of his right hand, he dismissed my questions. "Now is not the time to discuss such business. Perhaps, if you have some time this evening, we may return to my rooms on Baker Street for a smoke, and we may talk in a more private setting."

After a delicious meal of lamb cutlets and tomato salad, we returned to 221B Baker Street, and over a smoke of a particularly good blend of Turkish swag, Holmes updated me on his current assignments.

"There have been rather diabolical developments over the course of the month, Watson. The deep freeze has not slowed the sinister from planning dire attacks upon our fair city," Holmes began, smoke wafting from his nostrils and pipe, forming little dancing spirits before dissipating in the cloudy air. Holmes told of thwarting an Irish plot to dynamite St Paul's Cathedral and protecting a visiting Roman ambassador from a deadly assassin.

"I have missed having you by my side over the past few weeks, Watson, but I know your role as doctor is just as important to the people of London," Holmes explained, and lit his third pipe of the hour.

"Holmes, I do my part to earn my living," I explained, "but surely I have not done close to the service you, yourself, have done for the Commonwealth."

"Ah," Holmes countered. "Never underestimate the skills of a medical man. You bring hope to those who are suffering, and even when you find deficiencies in providing relief to those afflicted, you bring a calming presence to the masses. Without such calm comes unrest, with unrest comes anger, with anger comes unprovoked violence. Never underestimate your powers, my dear Watson. You bring needed calm to a world on the brink."

I must admit I was taken aback by my friend's unwarranted praise. I was about to tell him that I felt he overrated my work as a cog in the machine of London, when our late evening was interrupted by a loud rapping at the door from the street below.

THE ADVENTURE OF THE PECULIAR PROVENANCE

Holmes and I quickly extinguished our pipes and rushed down the seventeen steps to the front door. We did not want the late night caller to awaken Mrs Hudson.

"Who the devil could it be at this hour?" I grumbled, as Holmes and I descended the stairs.

"I have learned, Watson, that often my most difficult cases are brought to me in the darkest hours of night. Rest assured, this will be no idle visitor."

When we reached the bottom of the steps, I discovered that Holmes was, as usual, correct. Holmes flung open the door to find a young, wide-eyed constable standing in the street. He was clearly in a mode of great panic: his brown eyes bulged, his shoulders hunched, and hands flew about in the air.

"Mr Holmes, thank God, thank God. You are here! Thank God! Thank God!"

"I am here, my good man," Holmes said in a calm voice meant to reassure the officer. "As is my good friend, Dr Watson."

"Dr Watson!" the constable interjected. "Yes! That is good! Yes! Yes!"

Holmes and I gave each other puzzling looks. The constable was deeply troubled, and I noticed what appeared to be stains of blood coating his left hand.

"What is the matter, young man?" Holmes asked, again in a most soothing tone of voice. "Perhaps you and your companion would like to join us inside?" Holmes said, gesturing to the driver of the growler parked in front of Holmes' residence.

"No time, Mr Holmes! No time! You have to come to the Yard sir! Rousseau insists!"

"The Yard? Rousseau?" my friend asked, his left eyebrow raised at the name of the inspector.

"Yes sir, Chief Inspector Rousseau sent me. There's been a robbery, and a murder!"

At this Holmes grabbed the constable's shoulder and walked him back to the waiting carriage. "We'd best accompany this constable to Scotland Yard, Watson. Quickly, let us make haste."

After we all clambered into the growler and the horses pulled us away from Baker Street, Holmes turned to the constable and said, "Pray, young man, tell us everything about this robbery and murder."

Chapter 2

As our carriage moved along the moonlit London streets, Holmes patiently calmed the young constable, whose name we learned was Bellows, and got the man talking by asking fairly routine questions, such as *What is your name? How long have you been on the force? Who is your partner?* This helped slow the officer's pulse and get him focused on his mission: returning Holmes to Scotland Yard and explaining why he was needed in the middle of the night.

I was quite impressed with Holmes and his show of what we physicians call bedside manners. I added doctor and physician to the list of career paths Holmes could have taken, and I wondered how much the practice of medicine would change if the detective focused his attention to illnesses of the body instead of the criminal mind.

"My apologies, Mr Holmes," Bellows stammered. "I've never had a man die in my arms, and it all happened so suddenly. He was just...dead."

"You've suffered through a great ordeal, constable," Holmes stated sympathetically. "Perhaps you could tell me how all of this came about."

The constable kept looking at his left hand and fidgeting, gliding his red stained fingers over his palm, as if he could magically make the scarlet stains disappear. He kept staring at his hand, not making eye contact with either Holmes or myself, as he began talking in a rather monotonous voice.

"We received word of a break-in at the residence of Sir Hardwick Wellington in Belgrave Square. He had smelled smoke coming from his study and wondered if the flames in the fireplace had not been fully extinguished. When he went to investigate, he caught a hooded man attempting to steal one of his gallery pieces, a charcoal drawing of King Edward III of some high value. Sir Hardwick tried to stop the thief. A fight broke out, and unfortunately, the drawing fell into the fireplace, where it caught fire and burned. The thief hit Sir Wellington on the front and back of the head, and as Sir Wellington called for help, the thief ran out the front door, into the night, before any servants could come to Wellington's assistance."

Here the officer paused, and I thought Holmes would press the man on details, but Holmes let Bellows catch his breath, so that he could continue his condensed version of events.

"When we arrived at the crime scene, Sir Wellington explained that when he fought his accoster, he believed he recognized the man. He believed the assailant was an artist by the name of Sheldon Liddle. We went to Mr Liddle's diggings, a studio room at a tenement in Marshall St. Inspector Rousseau banged on the door, and we were both surprised when Mr Liddle answered. He was dressed in a long, black coat, his hair was dishevelled, and he matched Sir Wellington's descriptions. Surprisingly, Mr Liddle invited us into his home. It was a rather empty studio, with a straw bed, a table, a few chairs, and several paintings strewn about. They were in various stages of completion.

"Rousseau confronted the man and told him of a break-in at the residence of Sir Wellington. Here Liddle surprised us both when he admitted right then and there that he had been the man to break into the Wellington house. He then removed a folded sheet of paper from his coat pocket and handed it to Inspector Rousseau. The inspector read the paper and suddenly looked stricken. He glared at Liddle, folded the paper, nodded, and gravely said, 'Please come with us.'"

"Liddle calmly said, 'Very well,' and the three of us exited the room. It was a first floor lodging, and the carriage was waiting out front. We were quickly walking to the wagon, when a loud bang was heard, the sound of a gunshot. Liddle cried out, spiralled around, and landed in my arms, clutching his chest. Rousseau leaped into the wagon, and I followed with the dying man. The horses bolted out into the night, heading for the hospital, but within a minute or so, Liddle was dead."

"He was alive when the carriage started?" Holmes asked quietly.

"Oh yes...he was sputtering...gurgling blood...then he was gone. Rousseau ordered us to return to the Yard, and to bring him in quietly, keeping the body upright, as if he was alive and staggering like a drunk. I did what I was told. We brought him in, and my arm, my uniform, was coated in his blood. I had to change, and I was sent out to get you, with strict orders not to tell anyone what happened. I had to hide the truth, but my hand, it is still blood stained. I can still feel the life seeping out of him...so much blood … so much blood …." Bellows sniffled, and then broke down in loud sobs.

Holmes and I tried our best to reassure the officer that he did his job and that the death was not his fault. We finally were able to calm him, and we rode in silence the rest of the way to the Yard. Although quiet, I wanted Holmes to question the young man. So much of Constable Bellows' story had gaps. How did the thief enter Wellington's home? How did Wellington know the perpetrator if he was masked? How did he know the man's address? How did Liddle get shot in the middle of the night from an unknown assailant? And, of course, what did the letter say which Liddle gave to Rousseau?

I kept my tongue still until we arrived at Scotland Yard. After the carriage dropped us off, Bellows walked ahead of us to the brick entryway. I stayed back a moment with Holmes and whispered to him, "What is this about, Holmes? There are so many holes of logic in Bellows' story."

"Patience, Watson," my friend whispered in return. "The man is distraught, and I'm afraid that if I had pressed him, he would have completely unravelled. We should learn much inside," he concluded, and we both entered the newly built New Scotland Yard.

No sooner had we set foot in the austere building than we heard a rather loud call, "Holmes! So good of you to come down at this witching hour." Striding towards us was the white-haired Inspector Rousseau. "Ah, and I see you've brought Dr Watson as well. Sorry to bother you over a matter of paperwork," he concluded as he reached us. He grabbed Holmes by the left arm and pulled the great detective forward, almost knocking Holmes off his feet.

"Laying it on a bit thick," Holmes muttered.

"Quiet," Rousseau stated sharply. "I'll explain everything in a moment."

Rousseau led Holmes, Bellows, and me down the stairs to a holding cell on the basement floor. In the back of the cell was a blanketed, sleeping man. I quickly surmised that this must be the body of Mr Liddle.

"Has Bellows explained the situation?" Rousseau asked, still keeping his voice down.

"As best he can," Holmes answered and looked over at the constable who was standing at the iron cell bars, silently looking at the body hidden below the wool blanket and straw.

Rousseau nodded. "Queerest thing, Mr Holmes. A break-in, a murder, and then this," Rousseau pulled a folded paper from his uniform pocket and handed it to Holmes.

The detective opened it up, his features turning grim and his grey eyes hardening as he read the words on the page. He then handed the letter to me, and I almost dropped it from my hand. It contained the impossible.

Chapter 3

To whom it may concern,

The bearer of this letter, Mr Franklin Liddle, is hereby employed by the Secret Service of her Royal Majesty Queen Victoria, and is on a special assignment for the British government. By Royal Decree, let it be known that should Mr Liddle break any laws while completing work of a most delicate nature, he is absolved of any wrongdoing. Officers of the law should not restrict Mr Liddle from completing such work even if it seems contrary to your sworn duty. Interfering with Mr Liddle's aforementioned work may result in your own incarceration and possible execution.

Signed,

Mycroft Holmes

The paper was topped with the seal of Windsor Castle. The writing seemed authentic, yet for Mycroft Holmes to give a man carte blanche to commit crimes, even if supposedly in the line of duty, seemed unfeasible.

"Is this true?" asked Rousseau. "Is there some kind of secret service to the Queen which employs your brother?"

Holmes was pensive. He looked towards the ground, holding his chin between his right index finger and thumb. His mouth was in a deep frown as he contemplated the letter and the situation.

"I am not entirely sure," Holmes responded. "It seems most likely a forgery, yet the stock of the paper, the seal, and the writing appear authentic. I know of no such service to the Queen, yet there is much in my brother's dealings of which I have no knowledge. May we have a look at the body?" Holmes asked Rousseau.

Flustered by Holmes' answer to his question, the bewhiskered inspector merely waved his left hand towards the body. Holmes and I entered the cell, and I carefully removed the drape from over the body, revealing a rather dapper gentleman killed at the prime of his life. His auburn hair was slightly long and curly his pale blue eyes were glazed over; and his rigid facial features were frozen in a ghastly state of oblivion.

We turned the body over carefully, and delicately removed Liddle's coat. The collared shirt below was drenched in blood. It took another minute to remove the shirt and undergarments.

"Do you see the skill in this shot Watson? The bullet passed through the back of the man, bypassing the shoulder blade, cutting between the second and third rib, and then impacting the heart, probably in the left ventricle, causing the projectile to burst and rupture the heart."

I agreed with my friend's analysis. I also knew from my time in the service that it would take a skilled marksman to hit this shot in broad daylight, but at night, merely by the light of the moon and possibly a nearby gaslight, it would take a man of almost inhuman ability. This feat seemed to fit more in Professor Hoffman's *Modern Magic* than within the capabilities of a normal Homo sapien.

As if reading my thoughts, Rousseau sharply stated, "It would take a devil to make a shot like that."

"Or a man with the skills and motives of a devil," Holmes responded, still staring down at the body. "Inspector, how many people know about the condition of Mr Liddle?"

"Very few, just myself, Bellows, and the driver, Constable Quarterman. After reading the letter, I had the two officers bring Liddle in through the rear entrance and keep him upright, to appear alive and in a drunken stupor. I wasn't sure what to do, and if the letter was truly authentic, the less officers involved, the less of my force that may end up in the gallows," concluded Rousseau with a shake of his head and a long sigh.

"And you are certain no one else knows?" Holmes pressed.

Here Rousseau's ire was raised. "Mr Holmes, I know you do not think much of my force, but we are good men and solve most of the crimes of London with no assistance from you or anyone like you. My men are steadfast and honest. They have told no one, nor have I."

"I meant no disrespect," Holmes stated almost apologetically. "I merely had to be certain. Very well then, we have much work to do before morning. I have but one favour to ask."

"Name it," answered Rousseau.

"Dr Watson has a busy schedule tomorrow morning. He needs adequate rest. Could one of your constables give him a lift to his home?"

Holmes turned to me, seeing that I was about to protest. "There is nothing more for you to do here this evening, Watson. Return to your wife, tend to your patients, and return to 221B tomorrow afternoon."

I saw that, as usual, my friend was correct in his logic and reasoning. I agreed and soon found myself in a carriage being moved across the cobblestones of the city streets. While riding along, I wondered about the letter, the body of Mr Liddle, and what Holmes and Rousseau would continue to do that evening. I had to ask myself, could this be a case that would be too much even for the mind of Sherlock Holmes?

Chapter 4

I had feared that when I returned to my home, my brain would reject the state of slumber as I reflected on the confounding letter from Mycroft, and the gruesome marksmanship which had taken the life of the artist, Mr Sheldon Liddle. Despite my reservations, when I entered my home and went straight to bed, the Sandman covered me in his dust, and I woke the next morning fully rested.

In fact, as I supped my breakfast and read *The Daily Times*, I kept reflecting on an idea which had entered my brain upon waking. There is something to be said for the logic of Sherlock Holmes, but there is also something to be said for the magic which occurs when one slumbers. A tangled web of ideas can become clear after a short catnap, and a serious dilemma can be settled on occasion after a good night's sleep.

When I awakened, the image that came to my mind was not that of Sheldon Liddle, nor even of Mycroft Holmes. I woke with the image of Brigadier Charles Victor in my mind. Brigadier Victor, like myself, had been a member of the 66th Regiment of Foot, though he had retired before the dreadful Battle of Maiwand. I thought of Victor for two reasons. First, he was considered the finest shot in the Regiment. His shooting of a shilling, tossed into the air, from a distance of 1,500 yards was legendary. Second, the man was noted as a ranking member of the National Rifle Association. It was possible that he would have an idea of the man responsible for the murder of Mr Liddle.

THE ADVENTURE OF THE PECULIAR PROVENANCE

I remembered that, like many former members of the military, Brigadier Victor was now a commissionaire, having seen him quite by accident over a year ago as he was making rounds, delivering messages. I quickly wrote him a letter asking if he would be available to join me for lunch the next day. I then gave my dear Mary a kiss on the cheek, and before heading out to the home of my first patient of the day, I posted the letter, and anxiously awaited my friend's reply.

By ten that morning, my old army friend had already answered. He was delighted to hear from me, made a joke or two about how much we must be growing in the waist instead of in height nowadays, and agreed to meet me for lunch; however, he had a position assisting security at the Langham Hotel on Tuesday and wished to meet me on Wednesday instead. The speed of the London mail system astounded me. Within a few hours of communication, we had settled on meeting up at Ye Olde Cheshire Cheese on Fleet Street at noon in two days.

When Stevens relieved me of my medical duties in the late morning, I bundled up, hailed a hansom, and headed straight for Baker Street. I could not wait to tell Holmes of my own idea for discovering the identity of Mr Liddle's killer.

It took a little longer than expected to get to Baker Street due to the heavy amount of afternoon traffic. Mrs Hudson, Holmes' landlady, answered the door when I arrived. "Martha, so nice to see you," I said and tipped my hat to her.

"It's good to see you too, John. You best come in, and get yourself out of the cold." Martha was a kind woman about ten years my senior. She had a grandmotherly air about her, and she made sure that Holmes was well taken care of, especially in my absence. "I've got some cleaning to tend to in the kitchen, I hope you don't mind if I don't announce you."

"Not at all, my dear," I assured her. "We will have to catch up when you are not so busy."

"Yes, I would like that," Martha agreed, glancing over at the kitchen. I could see she really wanted to get back to her work, so I did not linger any longer and made haste up the stairs to see my good friend. After a few quick raps on the door, Holmes bid me enter. He was sitting in his armchair, pipe in mouth, his violin was lying in its open case on the floor before him. "You just missed my playing of Mendelssohn in E minor. It is a common piece, but played adagio, it is rather satisfying to the ear and the mind."

"Then I assume you have news to tell of the Liddle case."

"Yes, there have been some very interesting developments."

"Well, I have an interesting development of my own." I sat down in my easy chair and told Holmes of my idea to meet with Brigadier Victor for lunch.

"Excellent, Watson," Holmes commended me after I finished explaining my plan. "You will be a fine detective yet. You are already far superior to most of London's police force." Holmes invited me to join him in having a glass of sherry. He then gave me an update on the Liddle case.

"Much has happened since we last spoke, my friend," Holmes began, leaning back in his chair. "When you left, I spent several hours working with Rousseau and Bellows on a plan of action. We created quite a charade to pass Liddle off as living."

"Living?" I asked, alarmed. "But Holmes, when I last saw the man, he was a stone cold corpse!"

"Ah, Watson, you forget my theatrical background. I noted how Bellows was of a similar height to Liddle. The two also shared some similar facial features. With a bit of makeup, a wig, and some fine new clothes, I had Bellows take on the role of Liddle. His state of shock only added to his performance. I daresay, even his police partners will not recognize the man as he stays in the cell this week."

"This week? Do you mean the poor man will stay in the cell a full seven days?"

"It's quite possible. Mycroft will not return from Paris until this weekend. Bellows has no immediate family and few friends. He will not be missed. The corpse of Mr Liddle has been moved to the morgue as an anonymous body for the time being. After our ruse is over, then we will put all to right, and let Liddle's relations know of his untimely death," Holmes concluded.

"Is this really necessary Holmes?" I asked. "It feels too deceptive to the poor man's relatives. Don't you think Mycroft will be even harder on Rousseau and Scotland Yard when he returns and finds out about this ploy? This may assure that Rousseau, and maybe even you, end up with your neck at the end of a rope!"

Here Holmes gave one of his odd silent laughs. "Watson, you assume that there is some truth to Mr Liddle's letter from my brother. In fact, I knew instantly when holding the note last night that it was a forgery."

Again, I was astonished by my friend's behaviour. "Holmes! You put an innocent man in jail. You have an inspector of the Yard in fear for his life, and you say nothing!" Without realizing it, I had stood up, my fists clenched in anger. I would have continued on in snapping at Holmes if not for a subtle knock on the sitting room door.

With his right index finger, Holmes pointed to the armchair I had risen from, and motioned for me to return to my seat. He then called, "Enter!" The door opened, and in walked Mrs Hudson, wearing an apron with smears of dust upon it. Martha had clearly been cleaning the oven.

"A letter just arrived for you, Mr Holmes," Martha said, and handed over the mail to Holmes, a print of her hand showing in dust upon the envelope.

"Thank you, Mrs Hudson," said Holmes, and he carefully tore open the letter.

"Nice to see you here again, Dr Watson. How is Mary?" Martha Hudson said to me most pleasantly. I believe she was amused by interrupting my shouting at Holmes. It probably felt to her just like the old days.

"Mary is quite well, thank you. She was asking about you the other day. I believe she is planning a get together of the ladies for tea."

Martha beamed. "Oh, that sounds wonderful, Doctor."

"What's this," Holmes shot out of his seat. "Why Watson, the game has taken yet another turn. This letter is from none other than Sir Hardwick Wellington. He wants to hire me to investigate the theft of the charcoal drawing."

"A waste of money," I noted dryly. "That case has been solved. We already know Liddle is responsible."

Holmes would have none of that. "Come Watson, grab your coat and join me. I assume that you have no plans for the remainder of the afternoon."

"Only to spend it in your company, Holmes," I grumbled. I was still perturbed by Holmes' incarceration of the innocent Bellows.

"Very good," Holmes answered, ignoring the dissatisfaction in my tone of voice. If we hurry now, we can catch the next train out of the Baker Street Station. It will be much quicker than taking a hansom at this hour."

I quickly grabbed my hat and coat, and I said a polite goodbye to Mrs Hudson. Having her two lodgers, one current and one former, running off on a case certainly must have felt like she was back in the 1880s. The slight sparkle in her eyes showed me she was reminiscing.

As Holmes and I bounded down the stairs and headed into the chilly afternoon air, I asked Holmes. "Alright, how the deuce did you know that letter from Mycroft was a fake?"

"All in good time," Holmes panted. We dashed down the road, through the pedestrians on the sidewalk. "We will have a long journey to Belgravia, and I have much to tell you on the train ride."

Chapter 5

Even in below zero degree temperatures, Baker Street Station was as busy as ever. Throngs of people exited and entered the underground, newspaper barkers stood on soapboxes shouting out sales of the afternoon editions, all classes of people intermingled from the elegant with top hats and flower scented colognes to those hunched over in mud splattered rags. The trains were packed, nearly bursting with passengers. Holmes and I barely squeezed into our train when the bell rang out, the doors closed, and the locomotive behemoth began slowly crawling ahead on its tracks, chugging towards Piccadilly.

While the train increased in speed and moved us to our first transfer, my mind wandered, overwhelmed by the raucous noise of the engines, the ugly grime of some passengers, and the combination of fruity scents and unclean body odours. I couldn't help but wonder if this was society's future fate; the loss of the elegance of the horse drawn carriage, replaced by noisy coal or steam powered buses and private carriages. Perhaps London would find its way with aerial transportation. I had read of experiments with vast balloon ships and wondered if perhaps, like birds, we would take to the skies. If man developed such power, would we use it responsibly? Would we use our abilities for altruistic or devious ends? Would we soar to the heavens like Daedalus or crash to the sea like Icarus?

"Watson," Holmes said sharply, snapping me back to the present. "We are at our transfer."

We changed trains at Piccadilly, which was equally busy with the throngs of the masses moving about. Then we began heading towards Victoria Station. Just as before, we were equally crammed into the train like tufts of cotton forced into the belly of a doll to ensure its proper firmness.

Over the din of the screeching steel and hum of conversation, Holmes stated rather loudly, "Watson, the letter from my brother, you asked how I knew it was a fake."

"Yes," I nearly shouted in agreement. "The paper, the writing, it all seemed authentic to me."

"It was an excellent replication," Holmes agreed, speaking at the top of his voice, "The weight of the paper, the seal from Windsor, the handwriting, and even Mycroft's signature were almost complete to perfection."

"Then what gave it away?" I bellowed.

"It was not any of the technical aspects, but the content of the writing itself."

"You mean, Mycroft would never excuse someone of their crimes."

Holmes burst out laughing. "Indeed, I know he would and has. He has persuaded the pardoning of crimes far worse than a bungled burglary."

I nodded and thought for a moment. What else within the document's contents could lead Holmes to know the piece as a fake? Then it dawned on me. "I've got it! Mycroft's assistance of the Queen. He works for the British Government, not the Royal Family."

Holmes lifted his left eyebrow, nodded, his lips in a deep, thoughtful frown. "I see you are using your reasoning skills. Excellent Watson, but incorrect. In our Empire, the government and monarchy are still too intertwined to ever be completely separated. And my brother has, at times, worked with the Monarchy precisely to save the British Government. You must remember those dark dealings in Whitechapel over a year ago."

"Of course, Holmes. How could anyone forget?"

"And," the detective continued. "You remember why I did not get involved?"

"Yes, you said your brother was taking care of it."

"And, indeed, he did," Holmes explained. "I never told you that in doing so, Mycroft protected the Queen and the entire Royal Family. The series of murders was a charade intended to get the commoners of London to rise up and overthrow Victoria."

At this shocking revelation, I noticed how the noise around us had dissipated. A woman in a warm fur coat, as well as an olive skinned, droopy-eyed beggar and his daughter, shifted away from us. This didn't faze Holmes in the least, and he continued his explanation of events at full volume.

"The murders were designed to embarrass the Royal Family and point suspicion towards Prince Albert. Rumours flew that Albert was visiting the prostitutes in the area and that he, or even Victoria herself, ordered the murders. One rumour said the murders were to cover up for Albert having a bastard child with one of the ladies of the evening. Absolute poppycock, but effective poppycock."

"How did Mycroft assist the Royal Family?"

THE ADVENTURE OF THE PECULIAR PROVENANCE

"By working with the police, undercover agents, and even the Royal Guard, Mycroft was able to do two things. First, he was able to crush the slander against Prince Albert and the Queen. He was able to destroy the false evidence pointing to the Royal Family's involvement of the crime, and using his own agents, threatened those people who, innocently enough, hear a rumour and begin spouting it off again as fact. Second, he was able to catch the anarchists responsible for the murders and bring them to a swift justice."

At this assertion, my eyes bugged out, and my jaw dropped open. "You mean to say that the Ripper murders are solved? That the man responsible has been brought to justice?"

"Men, Watson, all eight of them were brought to justice. My point here is to say that my brother is a master of working undercover to assure things he does not want discovered do not get discovered. To have him give a signed letter to a man that says the bearer of the letter is a secret agent of the Queen is so out of character as to be utterly ridiculous. If this service is truly secret, it would not be called a Secret Service in a letter that could be handed off to any officer of the law. If Liddle was indeed working for my brother, and he was hired to do an illicit act, such as rob a house, it would no doubt be understood that if he were caught, he would be on his own, without aid from any royal or government sources."

I started to respond to Holmes, paused, then started again, then stopped. My mind was jumping about, thinking of all that Holmes had revealed from the brave acts of his brother in saving the throne and therefore, the Commonwealth, to all that was implied by the letter being a fake. It meant there was some grand conspiracy at hand. Who gave Liddle this letter? Who shot him? What ends did this serve?

"I believe we shall begin to get the answers to your unstated questions," Holmes laughed. "We have arrived at Victoria Station."

We left the station and quickly walked along the streets of Belgravia. I wondered if Holmes would want to hire a hansom, but he seemed happy enough to move at a brisk pace.

"Why are you keeping Rousseau in the dark? Why have Constable Bellows pretending to be Mr Liddle?" I did not understand this part at all.

"It is best for the assassin to not know he hit his mark. My theatrical creation may be necessary to lure the killer out of the shadows. I also wish for Mycroft's views on this situation. I posted a letter to him this morning explaining the details of the Liddle case. When he returns from France, I may need my brother's assistance depending on how this mystery unravels."

As we walked among the marble columns and the grand terraces, I asked Holmes how Sir Wellington tied in with this rather elaborate knot of crime.

"I need facts before I can theorise. To speculate would be dangerous without information. I would make the same mistakes as Rousseau and Lestrade, bending facts to meet my theory instead of using facts to deduce a solution. Ah, here we are."

And we had impeccable timing, for when we arrived at the four story stucco mansion of Sir Wellington, the front door flung open and a rather dour, obese butler stood holding the door. The man's expression could not have been sourer if he had eaten a lemon. With his thick jowls and pug nose, he reminded me a bit of Boxer, the bulldog I used to own, which died soon after I moved in with Holmes. Out of the mansion's open doorway strolled a fully jacketed servant girl, with an elegant violet scarf wound tightly around her neck, a stylish hat sporting several colourful peacock feathers upon her head, and a long, chic wool dress, the epitome of high fashion. Her attire was well beyond the typical servant's attire, yet it was not the full furs and jewels that a member of the elite class would wear on a winter's day. Both Holmes and I stopped as the woman walked by us, and we politely removed our hats and gave a slight bow. The girl looked almost unnerved at seeing us and quickly continued on her way.

Chapter 6

Before the butler closed the front door of the Wellington Mansion, we approached and declared ourselves. The corpulent butler, a tall chap of over six feet, glowered when responding to us. "Sir Wellington," he stated in a deep, guttural tone of voice, "is expecting you." He then ushered us in, out of the cold, and brought us to a large study with a plush, leather sofa before a roaring fire.

"Make yourselves comfortable," the butler said, "Sir Wellington will be with you momentarily." Holmes and I had a seat, and the butler exited, his girth barely allowing his body to fit through the door which closed behind him. I thought Holmes and I would have a little chat in the luxurious sofa, but no sooner did the door close then Holmes sprang up, took out his magnifying glass from beneath his coat, and began looking closely around the fireplace, the windowsill, and even looking behind some of the portraits on the wall.

"What are you searching for?" I asked my friend, a bit perturbed at him for running about the room. It seemed uncouth to be rummaging through a gentleman's belongings.

"Watson, I cannot thank that servant enough for leaving me a few scant moments alone at the scene of the crime."

"You're sure this is the room? This is an awfully large house with, I'm sure, many studies."

"Of course, I'm sure," Holmes snapped in a hushed tone. I could tell I had insulted the man for questioning his skill. "The additional ash in the fireplace, bits of it ingrained in the carpet, the deep scuff marks on the floor, the slight tilt to some of the other portraits in the room, it all indicates a struggle. Plus, there is a portrait in every area of the room except the space on the wall which the desk faces. That is where the criminal took the portrait from and attempted to steal it."

"He made no such attempt, Mr Holmes," said Sir Wellington. I turned, surprised to see the owner of the house standing in the open doorway, his portly butler by his side. The man shuffled into the room using a silver, wolf-headed cane to assist with his balance. Sir Wellington was a contrast of high fashion and lowly features. His eyes seemed slightly larger than normal, giving the man an ichthyic quality. His nose was pointy and mouth thin, much like a rodent and his hunched shoulders and back along with his odd limp gave him an added air of a frog. This amalgamation of hideous creatures was tempered with his fine tailored suit coat and pants, his rather debonair necktie, his diamond studded cufflinks, and his sweeping elegant white hair. There was a bandage slightly above the man's left eye, covering up what was most definitely a large lump, or as they say in boxing clubs, a shiner.

"Mr Liddle was successful in his mission. He wanted to destroy my portrait, and by tossing it into the fireplace, he was successful." Sir Wellington had been limping towards Holmes as he said this, and when he finished, he stood before my friend, a full foot shorter than the detective. He made a slight bow to Holmes and then to me. "Sir Wellington, at your service."

"As you already know," said Holmes. "I am Sherlock Holmes, and this is my associate, Dr Watson." I stood, gave a slight bow to the gentleman, and returned to my seat; then, Holmes continued. "We were under the impression that Mr Liddle bungled his attempt to steal your portrait of King Edward III; now, you tell us that he intended to destroy the portrait. I am intrigued. Please explain what exactly happened here last night."

"I will tell you all Mr Holmes, but first I want to make certain that you are the detective that is portrayed in the stories of Dr Watson, that those are works more of nonfiction than fiction. Excuse me for a moment while I sit down." With assistance from his butler, Sir Wellington sat down at the carved oak chair by his desk, a well-crafted furnishing with an ivory top. He then lifted up his walking stick and placed it on his desktop.

Holmes appeared amused. "How may I prove my talents?"

"A very simple task, Mr Holmes," Wellington stated, and then he said. "This walking stick has been in my possession for many years. Have a look at it, and then do your voodoo reasoning and explain something about me that is not general knowledge, something you could not know from articles in the newspapers."

Holmes nodded, and strode over to the walking stick. He put his head very close to the silver wolf's head, sniffed it, and then slowly moved his eyes down the rosewood shaft. After completing his brief examination, the detective stood tall and began reciting an evaluation of Sir Wellington in a dry, emotionless voice. "You are Sir Hardwick Wellington, knighted at the age of 30, not for your own accord, but as a

THE ADVENTURE OF THE PECULIAR PROVENANCE

favour to your father. You were an aspiring artist, but due to your excessive drinking, you developed a twitch in your hands and could never develop the skills necessary to be renowned. You turned to the world of art, hoping for a prestigious position in one of London's galleries; however, due to your excessive drunkenness and ill temper, you could never secure such a position, even with your father's assistance. His reach only went so far. You then became a noted art dealer, an area where you excelled, though the career was considered lowly for someone of your position in life. This has brought shame and embarrassment to you and your family. You are a feared and hated man, frugal, a widower at a young age who never could secure a second marriage, though your servant girl satisfies you as a lover, a man abusive towards his staff, a man wishing to be held in high esteem who is largely isolated from the world, and that is what I have learned about you from glancing at your walking stick, Sir Wellington."

When Holmes was reciting the knowledge he gleaned from the wolf-headed walking stick, I observed a contrast in character. Wellington's butler's face turned ghastly pale. His bottom lip quivered, and he looked like he would be ill right in the study. On the other side of the room was Sir Wellington whose face contorted in a ghastly expression of rage. His teeth clenched, his top incisors jutted out slightly, giving him a vampiric quality, and his head shook with a twitch, his body attempting to contain his fury.

At Holmes's conclusion, the room was silent, the air thick with tension. I wasn't sure if Wellington would leap at my friend's throat, or if the butler would vomit on the floor.

Maybe both. I was about to say something, make a joke about Holmes' observations to try and leaven the atmosphere, but before I could say anything, a low, guttural sound emerged through the clenched teeth of Sir Wellington. It increased in volume, a beastly tribal sound from humanity's primal days. Then suddenly, the man burst into a bout of barking laughter.

Both the butler and I looked at Wellington quizzically. And the butler asked, "Sir, are you all right?"

"Of course, Ronald, you damn fool. This man has just proved his worth. He deserves every shilling I intend to pay him."

The butler, apparently Ronald was his name, looked stricken, closed his mouth, and gave a pitiful nod of compliance.

"Now, Mr Holmes, I see you do have some magic about yourself. No, don't disagree. That's a lot to take from a walking stick, so now tell me, how did you learn so much from so little?"

My companion gave a nod of his head and explained. "First, I noted that the head of the walking stick was not only polished, but worn down, smooth, yet uneven, like a rock left out in the waves of the sea. This could only have come from a slight and steady twitch of the hand. What could cause that twitch? A number of possibilities exist, but because it is irregular, I surmised it was a twitch from alcohol abuse. I then noted the opulence of your cane. It is rather flashy and excessive, designed to show off the owner's wealth. Only a person who felt compelled to let the world know of their status would use such a cane, indicating that you are a largely forgotten man in your circles. Those who are knighted on their own merits are often remembered; those knighted for favours are oft forgotten. This led to my conclusion that your well-regarded father assured your knighthood, yet you could not rise to the level of your title.

"While the cane is jewel encrusted, I noted that some of the smaller diamonds have been refastened and there are two spots where small gems are now missing. Since you clearly have the wealth to replace them, this shows a frugality on your part. The dents in the bottom of the shaft come not from excessive weight bearing down on the shaft, but from the shaft smacking against something at an angle, in other words, from striking something, or in your case, someone.

"I noted that your servant girl who left tightened up her scarf as we walked by her, a common reflex of someone trying to cover up bruises. Your temper, I surmise, is well known to those who are close to you or get close to you, which is one of the reasons you cannot secure a second wife. No one who has a choice would tolerate your bruising blows, which is why your servant girl is also your lover. The fine clothes that she wears are enough for her to tolerate your temper and your advances. Now that I have concluded your test, perhaps you could get on, and tell us why you are hiring me to solve a mystery which, to the best of my knowledge, has already been solved by the Yard."

Wellington let out a deep, booming chuckle. "You are a sharp man, Mr Holmes. Though I think you cheated a bit by mentioning the bruises on Lucille, well earned, they were, as you'll hear in a minute. You were supposed to stick with the cane itself."

Holmes was about to respond that he did stick to the cane and just presented evidence which led to logical deductions, but Wellington cut him off before he could talk. "Bah," Wellington scoffed. "No matter. You passed the test, and since my secrets are out ..." He paused and nodded at Ronald. The butler walked over to the liquor cabinet, pulled out a decanter of scotch, and poured Wellington a full glass. I was shocked to see him deliver not only the glass, but the remainder of the decanter to his master. "Thank you, Ronald. That will be all."

The portly butler gave a bow and then left the room, leaving the three of us alone. "Never quite sure who I can trust," grumbled Wellington. "He's the best of the lot," he stated matter-of-factly referring to Ronald, "but he still could be working against me."

Wellington gulped his scotch, and then poured himself another full glass. "You will find, Mr Holmes, that there is much more to the story than just a meagre break-in attempt."

"Please start from the beginning," asked Holmes, and after another swig, Sir Wellington began his tale.

Chapter 7

"As you know, despite my less than honourable job title, I am a respected and noted dealer in works of art," started Sir Wellington. "Many a Stubbs, Romney, and Monet have passed through my hands into galleries, museums, and the homes of the aristocracy. While I earn my living as a broker of sorts, I also enjoy my own private collection. As you can see, this room is my portrait gallery."

Wellington paused to take another gulp of scotch, and I looked around the room for a moment. I had noted that the paintings in the room were all of posed men. One I recognized as the American Benjamin Franklin, another as our great statesman and Prime Minister, Sir Robert Peel, but many were portraits of people from the Renaissance to which I had no historical knowledge.

"At the beginning of the new year, I was approached by Mr Melvin Gregory, a curator of the National Portrait Gallery. The Gallery is currently housed in the Bethnal Green Museum in London's East Side.

"Gregory informed me that the Gallery was in the process of raising additional funds to move to its new location in St. Martin's Place. They had acquired a donation of a charcoal drawing of King Edward III, a rare piece from the 14th century. He inquired if I might consider purchasing the piece for my private collection. A charcoal piece from before the 16th century is rare, so I couldn't resist having a look, even if

Gregory's requests were odd. Bah! I should have seen through it all then, but my greed got the best of me."

"May I ask, what were Mr Gregory's odd requests?" Holmes inquired. He was now sitting beside me on the sofa, his eyes half open, his back stiff and upright, taking in Wellington's every word. Holmes' hands rested upon his knees, palms facing upwards, as if he was a Buddhist in a state of meditation.

Wellington nodded. "Of course, Mr Holmes. Gregory insisted that I meet him in his private office at the museum and that I tell no one about this, not even Sir George Scharf, the director of the National Gallery with whom I have had a working relationship for years.

"Now, you see, if I had made the request to tell no one that would have been quite normal, as I would want to have exclusive rights to bid on the portrait, but for the broker to make this request, that is highly unusual. Plus, if the money would go to the National Gallery, why would the director not already be informed?

"Of course, since my interest was piqued, and I knew that the Gallery was raising funds to get their own building in the centre of London, so they can move away from their current, dreadful location in the Bethnal Green Museum, which has leaky roofs which had allowed some of their paintings to get damaged, I put all questions out of my mind and decided to see this portrait of King Edward III."

"Before you continue," interrupted Holmes. "Do you still have the letter from Mr Gregory with his odd requests?"

"Yes, Mr Holmes, one moment." Wellington removed a key from his left vest pocket and unlocked the top drawer of his desk. He removed a small stack of letters. "I have them all, Mr Holmes. Here is every single letter from our brief correspondence."

Holmes walked over to the desk, opened one of the letters, read through it, and inspected it carefully. "I will need to keep these for the time being."

"Anything you need to catch that wretch!" Sir Wellington spat.

"Yes, pray continue your narrative," said Holmes as he sat back down resuming his palms up position. "Spare no details."

"Very well," continued Sir Wellington. "After I received the first letter, we corresponded back and forth a bit, and then we decided upon meeting on Sunday, January 19th. Again, I found it odd that he wanted to meet when the museum was closed to the public. But I had to see this piece, you understand, and when I did, I was not disappointed.

"I had my private coach readied, and on that brisk morning, we crossed London, swerved around the church-going traffic, and arrived at the door of the Bethnal Green Museum.

"In front, awaiting me, was Mr Gregory. He wore a full parka and a thick wool hat. The grey scarf around his neck made it difficult to see his facial features, yet I could tell the man was nervous."

"How so?" inquired Holmes.

"The pile of cigarette ash at his feet must have been from a good half dozen smokes. We all have our vices, Mr Holmes. It would be the equivalent of me having a full bottle of Merlot before a meeting."

Holmes joyfully beamed at Wellington's explanation. "Well said, Mr Wellington. You may have a touch of the detective in you. Pray continue your tale."

"After Gregory and I shook hands and introduced ourselves, he brought me into the cold iron and glass building. After a stroll through the main gallery, he brought me to his office. There, he unveiled the charcoal portrait to me, and what a find it was. For its age, the piece was in excellent shape, though some flaking had occurred, it was not excessive, and the canvas, though faded in parts, was also in fine condition. The picture showed King Edward with his flowing white hair, pointed beard, and moustache, but there was detail not seen in any surviving works on the subject. The man had deep wrinkles under his eyes and a heavy droop to his lids. This was the artistic find of the century.

"I inspected the provenance of the work and-"

"Just a moment," Holmes interrupted. His eyes were squinted, and he raised up his left hand as if he was a schoolboy in a classroom. "Did you or Mr Gregory suggest that you read over the provenance?"

Wellington ground his teeth for a moment, mulling it over. "Now that you ask, it was Gregory. I was so enrapt by the portrait, taken in, mind you, that I didn't even think of asking, but Gregory insisted on going to the library to check the work's authenticity."

"A provenance," Holmes turned and explained to me, "is a chronological record of the ownership of a work of art. The more complete the provenance, the more likely the work of art is to be authentic." I nodded in my understanding, and Holmes asked Mr Wellington to continue his fascinating tale.

THE ADVENTURE OF THE PECULIAR PROVENANCE

"The provenance was simple yet detailed enough. In the early part of the 16th century, the drawing found its way into a monastery in Dalmatia. The monks at the abbey treated the piece with a gum bath to prevent further flaking, and the portrait was sealed away in storage for a number of centuries. The work was rediscovered a decade ago, and the Gallery acquired the work in 1887. The plan was to have the piece as one of the works on display when the new museum opens; however, cost overages for the new museum created a funding shortfall of £5,000. To save both the museum and the Royal Family the embarrassment of publicly having to reach out for additional funds, I could acquire the piece for the said amount if I agreed not to unveil the work for one calendar year.

"Of course, I did, fool that I was," growled Wellington. "No sooner had I heard Gregory's demands then my cheque book was out of my pocket, a bill of sale was generated, and I left that day with the portrait in my carriage."

"Is that unusual," I inquired, "to complete a sale in such a rushed fashion?"

"Unusual, yes, but certainly not unheard of, Dr Watson. Most art pieces go to auction or more formal channels, but what did I care? I had the portrait. The price was steep, but for a work this grand, it was also fair. I brought the drawing to this room, made some adjustments, and found a spot out of direct sunlight and away from the fire. While I was supposed to not unveil the work for a year, I could not keep my pièce de résistance completely hidden from view, and so I chose this study, my own private one, knowing I could conduct my personal and private business elsewhere, and could enjoy the image of King George, myself, even if the world had to wait."

"How many others knew of your purchase?" asked Holmes.

"Just the staff here, no one of any importance, or so I wrongly thought," answered Wellington gruffly. "This is where that scoundrel Liddle enters the story."

Chapter 8

Sir Wellington finished his decanter of scotch with a swig. He had enough alcohol in his system that his face now reddened, his hands quivered, and there was a slight slur to his speech. "When the storytelling outlasts the bottle, I know I've spoken too long, yet I have so much more to say. Bah! There's my luck. I'm sure my anger will get me through this."

"Pray continue," said Holmes, and then as a reminder to Sir Wellington added, "you were about to explain Mr Liddle's role in this affair."

"Ah yes," slurred Sir Wellington. "But I am getting ahead of myself. After I took the portrait to my home and put it on display, I kept admiring the piece, and doubts began to enter my mind. The piece seemed too pristine for its age, especially since the drawing existed for over a hundred years before it was preserved. I kept my word and did not put the piece on public display, but I began making inquiries into art forgeries. How is it done? What are known fakes? I learned all about aging techniques, how to look for fake lines, checking materials, etc… Still, with this particular piece, it would be difficult to tell the fake. The artist was unknown. The style fit the time period. It looked old…and yet, I had convinced myself that it was a fake. But I needed evidence before I could challenge Gregory. I did not want to go back on my word until I knew for certain this piece was not genuine. After that, I would expose Gregory for his lies."

"From what you've said, it would be difficult to prove the piece was a fake. You saw the provenance," I stated.

"That is true Dr Watson. I had worked with a number of art experts over the years who authenticated pieces; however, there is one expert in particular renowned for catching art forgers: Professor Hermes Stapleton, an Oxford man. I contacted him, and he agreed to come to my home and inspect the drawing. He also agreed to look into the provenance of the work, quite peculiar for a work of that age to have everything in order."

"When was Professor Stapleton to view the work?" asked Holmes.

"Originally, he was supposed to view the work tomorrow. I have since written to him and cancelled, for obvious reasons."

I noted a slight frown on Holmes' face. I knew he would have liked to consult the Professor, possibly even bring the expert to the Gallery to inspect the provenance. It was an ever so slight frown, and my friend quickly returned to his stone, emotionless face and continued asking questions in his matter-of-fact parlance. "How did Mr Liddle become aware of your King Edward?"

"Ah, yes, I was getting to that part. A few days ago, I noticed a young man hanging around in front of the house. I had seen the man a few times before, and I realized why he stuck out. I remember the lad was an artist of some limited talent. I had seen him at a few shows, but I could not remember the man's name. I asked Ronald about this loafer.

"'He is Lucille's new beau,' the butler told me, and he did not hide the disdain in his voice. 'Shall I shew him away?' he asked.

"I had no reason to stop Lucille from seeing the man as long as she continued getting her work done and also pleasing me when I fancied her. I then asked Ronald if he knew the young man's name, and he told me the name was Sheldon. That's when it came back to me. I remembered the young man was Sheldon Liddle."

"Weren't you suspicious?" I asked, surprised by Sir Wellington's nonchalance about the affairs of one of his staff members, particularly his own mistress. Holmes raised his right eyebrow and gave me a look indicating he wanted my silence.

"I was suspicious, Dr Watson," continued Wellington, "but not about the charcoal drawing. I assumed he was trying to weasel his way into my household to attain favouritism with me. Many an artist has tried to gain my trust so that I may assist in helping him rise in the world of London art. None has been successful. If Lucille wanted to have a bit of fun with the lad, I saw no harm in it."

I winced at the vulgarities of Wellington's words, but I stilled my tongue at the insistence of the detective.

"Anyway, this brings us to the night of the break-in. I was wandering about my home, you see, as I had been wont to do so since the affair began. I was thinking about my reputation, the loss of a significant sum of money, and how this puzzle would all come together."

Surprisingly, Holmes burst out laughing and clapped for Sir Wellington. "Very good, very good, Sir Wellington. Bravo!

Those who suffer insomnia over an unsolved mystery are few and far between. I apologize for this interruption, but it is always exciting when I discover a kindred spirit. Pray, continue your story."

Wellington was startled by my friend's outburst. He turned to me and gave me a look which asked, *Is this man in his right mind?*

A mirthful expression came upon my face, and I gave a few quick nods and tried not to laugh.

"I was walking past this study when I saw a slight glow of light from under the door, and smelled a touch of smoke. I had been in the study but once that day, in the morning, and worried that somehow some ashes had never smouldered out, and the flame had been rekindled, though after such a long period of time, I questioned how that could be.

"I opened the door and entered the room, not trying to be quiet. Standing before the fireplace, holding the portrait in his hands, and admiring it in the light of the fire, was Mr Liddle."

"Just a moment," interrupted Holmes. "How did you know it was Mr Liddle?"

"Bah!" grumbled Sir Wellington. "I'm getting ahead of myself again. I did not know at the time. The man had a full mask on his head, a cloth sack with eye slots removed. Besides that, he was dressed all in black with a long, dark overcoat covering most of his body, and even wore thick, black work gloves on his hands.

"'What is the meaning of this,' I inquired. The brute simply glared at me for a moment then tossed the canvas onto the flames. With a scream of pure horror I rushed as quickly as I could to the burning canvas. Liddle stopped me, grabbing my

THE ADVENTURE OF THE PECULIAR PROVENANCE

right arm and twirling me to face him. When I stood before him, I grabbed at his hood, and upturned it for a moment. That's when I saw his face for just a second in the light. The young man then hit me on the head," Wellington explained, pointing out the bandage covering his shiner. "I stumbled back and fell to the floor. I then felt another hit to the back of my head and lost consciousness. The rest you know from the police report."

"A very interesting story. Are you certain the window was closed and fastened that night?" asked Holmes.

"Of course. In this cold, I wouldn't have it opened."

"You did not see or hear anyone else near the window?"

"No. In fact as I fell to the ground, I saw the curtains closed across the window. I felt no breeze from the area."

Holmes nodded for a moment. "And how did Liddle gain entry into your house?"

Here, Wellington lifted up his walking stick. "That I discovered with a little investigating of my own. It didn't take long for Lucille to explain she had invited Liddle in that evening for a secret rendezvous. The saying *spare the rod, spoil the child* also, in my opinion, applies to servants as well as the lower classes. While Lucille was preparing for a bit of fun, Liddle snuck away to the study. He had asked her about the displayed paintings of my house and the portrait of King Edward. The simpleton had told him everything.

"After Liddle had knocked me to the floor, he simply ran out the front door. Ronald, with his weight, could not flee after the burglar, and so the man escaped into the night."

"Yes, yes, I see," nodded Holmes in agreement. "Now we come to the important question, what, exactly, are you hiring me to do?"

Here Sir Wellington answered in a rather sombre tone, "I would like the scoundrel Gregory revealed for his crimes. Catch the man, Mr Holmes. I'm certain the thread is lost on this case, though I'm sure there be others. Catch the man using the name of the museum to run his own lucrative scheme, for I'm sure that is what he is doing, using the name of the Portrait Gallery to swindle others and gain his own wealth. Bring the man to justice before the name of the museum, even the name of the Queen herself, is sullied. I only ask that when you have caught the crook, you let Sir Scharf and others of prominence know the small role I played in exposing Mr Gregory. As you've said, my family's name has a cloud of shame upon it. Let this act be my first in clearing the smog and restoring the Wellingtons to their former glory."

Holmes listened to the request, keeping his stoic visage. I admit, I was moved by Wellington's explanation, knowing what it is like to overcome family shame and dealing with my own private vices.

Finally, Holmes said, "I accept your case. We still need to discuss the matter of my fee."

Sir Wellington beamed. "I have that all figured out. The cost of the fake was £5,000. I feel your fee should be the same."

My eyes bulged at this announcement, and I had to keep from gasping aloud.

THE ADVENTURE OF THE PECULIAR PROVENANCE

Holmes simply nodded and agreed. "That shall be acceptable."

Chapter 9

We rode home in a fairly empty train car. As he was apt to do, Holmes did not discuss the case of Sir Wellington nor the murder of Mr Liddle, the two cases clearly intertwined, yet I could not see where the threads connected. Instead, Holmes lectured me on the great skill of the composer Max Bruch, and how his Violin Concertos are underrated, whereas Tchaikovsky's works are nothing more than sentimental drivel.

After we changed trains again at Piccadilly, we found ourselves returned to the crowded throngs of London packed within a car. Once the locomotive started chugging on its way, it was as if a lever in the mind of Holmes was switched, and his mind went from discussing music back to discussing Liddle's murder.

"I never told you that this morning I paid a visit to the room of Mr Liddle," began Holmes, his voice now slightly raspy for having to shout over the noise of the train car, though I thought he was being louder than necessary.

"What did you discover there? Could you make any headway into his murder?"

Holmes appeared delighted. "I discovered nothing, Watson. Nothing at all."

"Really, Holmes," I grumbled. "How can you appear so jolly at discovering nothing?"

"Because Watson, that, in and of itself, was discovering something."

"You're speaking in riddles, old man."

"Ah, yes, let me explain. When the constable on duty allowed me to enter the residence of Mr Liddle, I already had surmised what would greet me. The entire flat had been cleaned from top to bottom. Not a single finger print remained on a doorknob or utensil. The half completed paintings noted by Constable Bellows were missing. There was nothing left in the drab studio besides his worn furniture and plain table and chairs."

"But Holmes, how can that be? There was a constable on duty."

"Rousseau did not post a constable at the scene of the crime until after you had left the Yard last night. I am sure that when the police wagon carrying the injured Liddle fled the scene of the crime, the attacker and his other associates were already moving towards the flat to fumigate. By the time Bellows arrived at 221B to fetch us, I believe Liddle's studio had been sterilized."

"Why Holmes," I stammered, "this is beginning to sound like a vast conspiracy of crime one reads about in those penny dreadfuls."

"Indeed, Watson," Holmes agreed. "It does have the air of a well-crafted tale about it."

*

On our return to Baker Street Station, we said our goodbyes and parted. Holmes had some work to do involving other cases, and the hour was getting late. I planned on checking in with Stevens the next morning to make certain all was well with my medical practice, and then Holmes and I would rendezvous at the Bethnal Green Museum early in the afternoon. Holmes wanted to study the provenance of the King Edward III to see if he could find a flaw in the forgery and expose Mr Gregory's crime.

I was surprised when I awakened that next day to find I had received a letter from Holmes. He had taken it upon himself to get an early start and explore the National Portrait Gallery on his own; however, he had reserved a private room at Johnson's Tavern at noon, and asked me to meet him there for lunch. After spending a relaxing morning in the company of my wife, I went to my office and found Stevens busy but in high spirits. My patients were on the mend, and it seemed that the fevers that had grasped London were finally breaking.

At 11:30, I said my goodbye to Stevens and took a hansom to Johnson's Tavern. The establishment was not one regularly attended by Holmes, but the owner was in the detective's debt. Holmes had helped clear Johnson of an accusation of cheating at cards. My dear friend proved Johnson's innocence and asked for payment that the private room in the back of the bar, usually reserved for large social gatherings and the occasional tournament of poker, be at my friend's disposal at any time.

When I entered Johnson's, I was hit with a cloud of cigar smoke as thick as that of London's notorious fogs. The luncheon crowd was made up of elite business men making deals over smokes and brandy. Johnson greeted me himself. The pallid, lanky owner was even more rail thin than Holmes. He wore a debonair suit and ushered me into the private room in the back.

The room was clearly set up for a future match at cards, and I cursed my luck that my dear Mary had accepted a dinner invitation for us that evening to dine with an acquaintance and her husband. I'd much rather be showing off a royal flush than politely discussing my medical practice with people I barely knew. There were three round tables, each surrounded by six chairs, spread out in the room, as well as a few lounges in the corners. Holmes sat at the table in the centre of the room, puffing on his clay pipe, a glass of cognac before him. He pleasantly greeted Johnson and me. Johnson took our food orders and then left the room. Once the proprietor was gone, Holmes stopped his cheery act, and I could see from the tension in his shoulders and frustration in his eyes that things did not go well at the Gallery.

"They are a clever group, these thieves, leaving absolutely no trace of their dealings," Holmes began. "I went to the museum today dressed as Cecil Meddleton, a facade I've used on occasion when I have needed to look at scholarly documents in galleries. Through the assistance of Mycroft, Meddleton's credentials are well known throughout the world, so it was no problem to get access to the library's collection of provenances.

"I brought the letters which Gregory had sent to Wellington. While I knew that the provenance from the King Edward would be missing, I hoped to find a trace of forgery somewhere else in the historical sources. I found no evidence of tampering, at least not by the hand of Gregory."

"Was there any other forgery you discovered? Any forged art on the gallery walls that perhaps could lead back to Gregory?"

Holmes let out a plume of pipe smoke and shook his head, his frown deep and grey eyes dour. "The problem with an eye like mine in an art gallery is that the forgeries distract from the true works of beauty."

"Whatever do you mean, Holmes?"

"I mean, dear Watson, that when I enter a museum or gallery or another such establishment allowed to show off the aesthetics created at the hand of man or works from the origins of our species, I note, at minimum, ten percent of the displayed works of art or primitive tools or original documents are complete and utter fakes."

"Really Holmes! Ten percent? Why if that was made public!" I stammered in shock.

"If that was made public, Dear Watson, it would cause a chain reaction leading to all ancient and historical works of art to be called into question. The value of art would plummet. Wealth would significantly decrease, leading to a chain reaction ending in a deep, global financial recession."

"That is why you do not bring this information forward?" I asked, still stunned at this news.

Holmes chuckled. "You know my brother. Even if I tried, he'd prevent it from happening, which I'm sure he already has on other occasions when other individuals have attempted to bring this information to light."

We paused in discussion as Johnson knocked on the door. We welcomed the ghostly figure in, and he put our plates of fried fish and mushy peas on the card table, and asked if we'd like anything else. We thanked the man and dismissed him. While we dined, I asked Holmes what his next steps on the case would be.

"I need a few hours with my violin this afternoon before I can say for certain. I also look forward to hearing the information you glean from your friend on the best of Britain's marksmen. While I am vexed with the pace of this case, I assumed it would be complete in twenty-four hours' time, it still has a limited number of conclusions. We shall continue on, Watson, and will bring all factions of this case to a close in due time. Now, let us enjoy this fine meal."

"Oh," I remembered, at the mention of good food, "I have a request from Mary."

"Yes?"

"She wishes to have you and Mrs Hudson over for dinner tomorrow evening. She was most insistent that Martha accompany you as well."

"Why, that's excellent," Holmes said, and his sullen expression lightened. "It will give us an opportunity to exchange notes, and it will give Mrs Hudson a much needed respite from her work in the kitchen."

I was thrilled to hear that Holmes accepted the invitation, and I believed Martha would join him. Still, I wondered, why was Mary so insistent that Martha accompany Holmes?

Chapter 10

After my dinner engagement with Mary's friends, I returned home and had a restful night's slumber. So much so that when I awakened, the sun was much higher in the sky than I anticipated. My dear Mary chastised me by saying, "This proves how overworked you are. You must take better care of yourself when you return to your practice tomorrow. No more fourteen hour days!" I nodded in agreement. I find that if in a hurry, it is always better to acquiesce with my wife than to make an argument. If my duty to my patients requires me to work a full 24 hours, then that is what I must do. I kept my tongue still, though, and just responded with sweet reassurances.

I barely had time to browse *The Times* and drink a cup of coffee before it was time for me to rendezvous with Brigadier Victor. I hired a hansom and just arrived at Ye Olde Cheshire Cheese when the sun was declaring the noon hour. It had been over a full year since I had seen Brigadier Charles Victor, but I think if it had been twenty years, I still would have recognized the chap.

He was sitting in one of the small wooden booths on the chop house side of the establishment, his moustache, now more grey than black, was twirled up at the ends, and his regiment training showed by the man sitting stiffly, like a rod was attached to his spine, always keeping his head up with not the slightest hunch about him. He was wearing his commissionaire's uniform, its red woven chest front and cuffs made him stand out like a rooster in a brood of hens.

"John," my old friend called and stood up. I went to shake his hand, but the burly fellow was so excited to see me, he gave me a big hug, and I felt myself lifted off the ground for a moment. He then slapped me on the back, "Jolly good to see you, old chap. Jolly good." Although Charles had joked with me about growing in the waist, the man was still a pile of muscle below his newly formed layer of fat. I felt a bit awkward for I knew my physique had fallen away compared to my lunch companion.

We spent a brief time catching up, since it had been a few years. I told him of my marriage to Mary, my medical practice, and my work with Sherlock Holmes.

"I heard something about that," the gruff commissionaire said. "You wrote a book, didn't you? Something about the police taking all the credit for your friend's work."

I chuckled at this summary of my novel, *A Study in Scarlet*.

"I don't doubt that your version of the story is closer to the truth than the one that came out in the papers," Victor continued. "Giving Lestrade and Gregson all the credit, wot! I know those two. Those publicity hounds find ways to make simple cases as complex as possible, just to get themselves a little press. Are those two involved in this case, whatever it is?"

I carefully retold the case, but I framed it as a story around my medical practice. I said a man came to me with a shoulder wound and said he believed a man shot him from a considerable distance, in the evening, from the roof of a six floor tenement building. I described the general conditions of

Mr Liddle's murder but with a man who survived and claimed it was a shooter hired by one of a list of angry tenants he had evicted over the years.

"Let me guess," Victor sneered. "The Yarders said it couldn't be done. Granted, the story has a bit of a fish tale in it. That's a lot of trouble to go to because of losing your flat. If this patient of yours is telling the truth, mind you, he is leaving out a good chunk of the back story. This sounds like a mystery for that Holmes fellow you run around with."

"That's why I came to you, Charles. How many men would be capable of striking a man at that distance in the dead of night by no more than the murky gaslight on a nearby pole?"

Charles sat back for a moment, mulling it over. "It's difficult to say, John. First you are assuming that the shooter was aiming for the arm. There's a good chance he really wanted to hit him in the head or the heart. But, let's just say you are correct and the shooter was aiming to clip the man, just to send a message. There's more than distance to look at here. You've got the angle of the shot, the fact the target was moving when he was shot; also, I am guessing that the rifle had a silencing device on it, otherwise, the whole tenement would have awakened."

"A silencing device?" I inquired.

"Oh yes. They are still in the experimental stage, and no one has commercially manufactured them, but I know a few chaps who are part of the National Rifle Association who have been tinkering around with the devices. They add an extension tube to the muzzle of the rifle. One of the blokes I know uses one that looks like a tin can. Anyway, it makes for a much quieter discharge. My guess is if someone awakened to the noise of the shot, they'd think it was some bookcase falling to the ground or a turned over carriage, or some other calamity which would cause such racket. Something loud, but not something to be worried about, that's why no one in the tenement building investigated the noise."

I saw the logic in Victor's reasoning, and thought that this could be a bit of luck in helping us catch the killer. If a silencing device was used, then this could significantly reduce the number of suspects.

"There have been so many advances in weaponry as of late that it is hard to keep up with the pace and ease we are making of exterminating each other," Victor added, coldly. "With the cordite, the faster bullets, the automatic rifles, mark my word, John, the next war will bring about hell on earth."

His gruesome depiction of the future returned my mind to the horrors I witnessed in Maiwand, and I said, my voice quivering, "Let us hope that this new age of glorious inventions brings mankind closer together, not further apart."

Victor slowly nodded his head, and we sat in silence for a moment, both our minds reflecting back to the savagery of the battlefield. Then, Victor surprised me by saying matter-of-factly, "It will be difficult for you to catch this criminal. Yes, doctor, I can tell you've not been completely forthcoming with me, and that this is a case for Sherlock Holmes. No matter, I understand and perhaps you are protecting me. Even so, if I give you the names of the dozen or so men I know that are tinkering with this invention, I think you will find that they are men of significant prominence."

"There is no such status in the eyes of the law."

Victor let out a low growl. "If only that were true, John." Here, my friend took from his pocket a three inch metal tube I recognized as a police whistle. "They let me keep one of these for my security jobs. I've had to use it a number of times. Working in the hotel business, you wouldn't believe the sickening sights I've witnessed that occur when the gentry close and lock their doors at night. Some of those not so high on the status scale have had to pay for their crimes, most haven't. That's the way of the world, John. The rich have power beyond the eyes of the law."

I straightened my back and held my head up for a moment. "Sherlock Holmes levels that playing field. I often think he goes out of his way to take cases that indict the top echelon of the world. Men like Sherlock Holmes cut those brutes down to size. No one, not even one of royal birth, can hide from his reach."

Victor paused, reflected for a moment, and then gave a few quick nods of his head. "Very well. I will give you the names of the men I know. Mind you, we are talking some with royal blood, some military colonels. This is just my list. There are many more men out in the world who are not part of The National Rifle Association, inventors working on new weapons. There are certainly foreigners designing silencing devices as well. Mind you, these names may help, but I have a feeling not a single one would be shooting landlords from atop tenement buildings."

"Thank you, Victor. We will leave that for Sherlock Holmes to discover."

*

THE ADVENTURE OF THE PECULIAR PROVENANCE

Victor and I continued talking for another quarter hour. He was proud that Queen Victoria had indicated she would grant the National Rifle Association a Royal Charter. Their shooting competitions were increasing in popularity, and Victor believed he had a good chance of taking home a bronze medal. After we cleaned our plates, Victor saw the time and apologized for having to run off. He had deliveries to tend to, so we said our goodbyes, and I volunteered to cover the cost of our bill. Once Victor left, I sat alone for a moment, finishing off my ale. The thought of the grey haired former Brigadier captured in my mind, and I reflected that no matter how one lived his life, for good or ill, Time would eventually clutch us all and deliver every living creature to his brother, the Grim Reaper.

When I finished my last drop, I got up from my seat and saw below the table, Victor's police whistle. I picked it up and thought I'd dash after him to see if I could catch him on his rounds before he got too far. I left my payment on the table and quickly turned to leave, bumping into another patron. I apologized to the man but in that half second, the neurones in my brain connected, and I instantly recognized the chap. He was a well-dressed man with a dark, lengthy beard and olive skin. I don't know whether it was the tone of his skin or the crinkles around his eyes, but as I apologized, I instantly recognized the man as the gentleman who had been standing behind Holmes on our train ride to Victoria station when we made the acquaintance of Sir Wellington. I also noted that when we collided, the upper left corner of his beard slightly detached from his face. The man was in disguise, which meant this was no coincidence. The scoundrel was following me.

Once I composed myself, and the olive skinned man assured me that he was all right, I sauntered out the door, and at a fast pace, strolled down Fleet Street. I kept my feet moving briskly, almost at a jog, and I kept my eyes mostly forwards. At one point, I paused, looked down at my watch, and made a slight glance behind me. About twenty paces back was the bearded man, following me. I decided to reverse our roles and stayed in the centre of the sidewalk, adjusting my watch, pretending that it had stopped ticking. The olive skinned man walked past me, and after he had wandered a good twenty paces beyond me, I started following him. *Where was he going? Why was he following me? How was he involved in the murder?* I knew I may not find the answers to all of my questions by following the man, but I also knew, just by discovering his destination, that might be enough for Holmes to connect the dots and solve the crime.

Chapter 11

One does not work closely with Mr Holmes without learning a few tricks of his trade. As I followed the man with the fake beard, I made certain to stick as closely to crowds as possible, moving between them, yet maintaining the same pace as the man I was tailing. To make certain I wasn't moving too quickly nor too slowly, I kept my eyes at his feet and bobbed my head slightly to his foot step rhythm. I made certain to note my surroundings, but I also knew not to get so caught up in mapping out my route as to allow my target to slip away when I was distracted.

Tracking the man was not difficult. He was walking at a steady yet leisurely pace, wandering up Wine Office Court to Pinter. Every pub, shoppe, or residence we approached made me wonder if this establishment or home was to be the spy's rendezvous point. When he stopped in front of Ye Olde Mitre, that well known pub, I thought for certain that this would be the meeting point, and I would discover who had paid the man to follow Holmes and me. It was the perfect meeting spot, public and loud, allowing the fiends to hide in plain sight. The droopy-eyed fellow paused for a moment or two, his head shifting left to right as if he was looking for someone or something. I thought this meant that the man was indeed meeting an accomplice, who was perhaps running a bit late. No such luck on my part. After a short time, the fellow tapped on the edges of his fake beard, probably reassuring himself that it remained properly stuck to his face, and then he continued on his walk, strolling on past Ye Olde Mitre, towards Bleeding Heart Yard. We continued northward, through the gate at the north end of Ely Place.

As we ventured past Bleeding Heart, I noticed that we were the only two people on the cobblestone roads in the area, and that the droopy-eyed man's pace had quickened. I wondered if this meant my target was now worried, perhaps Ye Olde Mitre was his meeting place and his appointment had not shown, or worse yet, with his rushed pace, perhaps he was on to me. The problem with allowing my mind to wander, even if it was briefly, was that I was not paying attention to my subject. Even though this momentary distraction lasted a few mere seconds, when I double checked the bearded man's pace, I was shocked to see he was no longer in front of me; in fact, he was nowhere to be found. I raced ahead and looked around, but the street was empty. I double backed and eyed my surroundings. There was a small hotel, a jeweller's shoppe, some residences, but all had their doors closed. *Would I have missed him dodging into a home or business*? I wondered. I thought the sound of a door opening would have drawn my attention. There was an alleyway he could have dashed towards, and if he had done it stealthily, I decided, I may have missed him. The alley was wedged between the jeweller and the hotel. It was just wide enough for a hansom to fit through. I turned down the alley and found it deserted. I looked up at the brick walls and down at the cobblestones on the street, looked for any signs of a doorway the man could have hidden in, or a footprint left on a damp stone.

There were two doorways in the alley, one leading to the hotel and one to the jewellery shoppe. I checked the hotel and found the entryway deserted and the door locked. I ran over to investigate the jeweller's door. I found this doorway also empty, the door closed. I was about to leave when I turned and looked back at the jeweller's door. It was closed, but it was not shut all the way. I reached my hand to the doorknob when, suddenly, the door flew open, slamming into my body and knocking me backwards. I gave a brief howl of pain and saw a flash of colour as the man ran up to me and gave me a swift blow to my abdomen. I wheezed and crumpled to the ground. I tried to call for help, but found my voice gone, my body trying to take in deep breaths as I clutched my stomach.

"Such a fool, Dr Watson," the man addressed me. His speech was harsh, yet his tone was level, and his voice quiet. "Had you left me alone in the restaurant, had you pretended that you did not recognize me, I would have had no way of knowing that you did."

I was attempting to pull myself up off the ground at this point, and the droopy-eyed man gave me a swift kick to my gut. I groaned and fell back to the ground, not able to breathe.

"I'm not allowed to injure your companion, Sherlock Holmes. You, on the other hand, there's no rules about you."

The man, now sans beard, looked down at me, his eyes glowing in a malicious flame. He had something in his right hand now, my eyes were a little blurry, but I could see it was a knife of some sort. Then I rolled away as best I could. I didn't have the strength to get up off the ground, but I knew I had to flee. Even in my sad state, I recognized his weapon as that of a stiletto, that swift thin blade preferred by assassins throughout the ages.

My ears detected the sound of distant chatter and laughter. Someone was in the nearby vicinity. Someone could come to my aid. Yet, I couldn't call to them. My voice would not work. Then, I remembered. I felt a metal tube in my pocket. I had Victor's police whistle.

The olive skinned assassin moved silently toward me, his blade ready to strike. I knew he had heard the calls of the nearby pedestrians, and as he leaned over me, I knew the man intended to slit my throat. As my would be killer was about to grab my head, I quickly put the police whistle between my lips and blew into it, the noise staggering the man, as he was mere inches away when I blew the noise into his face. The man fell back, dazed by the noise, and suddenly we heard calls of, "You there. What's going on?" and the sounds of running footsteps on the street stones.

The droopy-eyed man stood up, and I blew the whistle again. The man glanced both ways, cursed under his breath, and dashed off, away from me, and away from my oncoming help.

*

An hour later, I found myself in the care of Scotland Yard with Rousseau at my side, his white hair tossed about in the frigid breeze.

"You're lucky to be alive, Dr Watson. From now on, you leave the detective work to the Yard."

I groaned and nodded in agreement. "I didn't know he was dangerous," I managed to wheeze. "I thought I was helping."

"Well," snapped Rousseau, "you'll be no help to anyone, especially that wife of yours, if you end up in a box six feet underground."

"Please," I begged the inspector. "Not a word of this to Mary."

Here Rousseau chuckled. "No worries there, friend. I won't worry your little missus. Best to leave women out of these sordid affairs. Since you were just beat up a bit, I can't imagine any papers would find this of interest, either. I believe you are in the clear."

"Inspector," a constable interrupted us. "We finished our search and found no evidence of any wrongdoing."

Shortly after I blew my whistle, help had arrived in the form of a group of two young couples who had been returning to their hotel rooms. They saw my assailant huddled over me, and when he left the scene of the crime, the two men in the group pursued him. They lost him just a few streets later. The women stayed with me, and checked to make sure I was all right. When the husbands returned from their ill pursuit of the droopy-eyed assassin, they helped me to my feet, and helped walk me to the hotel. The maître d'hôtel, a kindly man with a stiff upper lip, sent for the police. When Rousseau heard word at the Yard that I was the victim of an assault, he came, himself, along with several constables to make certain I was safe. He also sent a message to Holmes, but the detective was not at 221B Baker Street.

I gave a description of my assailant to the constables, and officers made inquiries both at the hotel and at the jeweller's. From what they could determine, the man had most likely known of the alley and may have even known that the jeweller normally keeps his door unlocked during business hours; however, it was determined that the jeweller was in no way involved in the crime nor were any patrons or employees of the hotel.

One of the Yard's medical men gave me a final check-up and determined what I had already surmised, that I was bruised and battered, but no bones were broken and no organs damaged. I was, quite frankly, very lucky to have come face to face with death and leave with only my body blackened and my ego bruised.

"There is nothing more for you to do here, doctor. Best get you home, so you can rest up. If we need to make further inquiries, we will contact you. I'll make sure we do it in a way so as not to arouse the suspicion of the missus," Rousseau added with a wide grin.

I thanked the man and his force for their aid. An officer was permitted to bring me to my home, using an unlabelled growler, so I did not show up at my home in the back of a police wagon, in the middle of the afternoon, stirring questions not only from my wife but from our neighbours.

As I sat in the growler, my body being jostled about by the quick pace of the driver and his horse, I found myself in a deep melancholic state. I had set out to discover the whereabouts of the villains in this tangled caper, and I ended up with no useful information to aid in the solving of these crimes. I had to dismally admit to myself a painful fact, a fact more painful than the agony felt by my body, a fact more distressing than the lashing taken by my self-esteem. With a tearful shake of my head, I acknowledged the plain truth; I had failed Sherlock Holmes.

Chapter 12

On my return to my home, I explained to Mary that I had stumbled down a set of stairs to account for my bruises, reassured her that I was sore but quite all right, and then rested on the couch in the sitting room. That evening, or rather later that afternoon, Holmes and Mrs Hudson arrived at our doorstep. I was still resting on the couch, tackling a word cross puzzle, while Mary was whiling away in the kitchen. I heard a sharp knock at the door and answered it to find the beaming smiles of both Holmes and Hudson. Martha brought cornucopias for dessert, and Holmes brought two bottles of sherry. They were both well dressed for the evening. Martha was wearing a lengthy, black dress, and a warm evening jacket. Holmes was in a debonair grey suit and tie.

I welcomed my two guests into the sitting room, and took their hats and coats. I offered for them to sit down, but before they had a chance, Mary emerged from the kitchen and warmly greeted Holmes and Mrs Hudson. "Martha, what wonderful cornucopias!" my wife exclaimed. "I have the cream we can add to them later."

"I hope that is not too much of a bother," Mrs Hudson said apologetically.

"Nonsense, nonsense. Let us away to the kitchen. There is so much that I need to show you," Mary said and clutched Martha Hudson's right arm, directing her to the kitchen.

"Is it really all it is cracked up to be?" Mrs Hudson asked, and I did not hear Mary's answer as the ladies disappeared into the noise of the kitchen.

"What the devil are those two on about?" I asked Holmes.

"Ah, I had thought Mary had told you," Holmes admitted. "Martha is considering purchasing a new gas stove to replace her coal burning one. She is thrifty when it comes to new purchases, but I believe your wife will persuade her. When Martha sees with her own eyes that she will no longer need to be up at dawn to haul coal inside to light the oven and get it warmed up, that should be enough to convince her. If that doesn't do it then the cleanliness of the gas stove will, no cleaning up the soot afterwards. Makes for a much tidier kitchen."

Once Holmes finished his explanation, his visage shifted to one of concern. "Watson, how are you? Rousseau told me everything, and I rushed Martha over as quickly as I could. She knows nothing of the events that transpired. I will give Rousseau credit. He knows how to keep secrets."

I nodded in agreement and winced as I felt a sharp pain in my gut. "My injuries, painful as they may be, are only surface injuries. I'll feel them for a few days, but they won't stop me from returning to work in the morning. Holmes, what pains me even more than these bruises is to admit how I have failed in assisting you on this case."

Holmes removed his clay pipe, added some tobacco, lit it, and, after taking in a few puffs, said, "I have a feeling you are underestimating your own powers of deduction. Let me hear of your day."

With that invitation, I told Holmes of everything I had learned from Brigadier Victor. I explained how I tailed the droopy-eyed man with the fake beard, my assault, and my rescue.

When I had finished, Holmes looked dreadfully serious. "It is good fortune that you had your friend's police whistle with you this afternoon, Watson. The Chief Inspector is correct. Leave the dangerous tasks to the police from here on out. How could I possibly go on without my Boswell?"

"I apologize for not bringing you any useful information beyond that told to me by Brigadier Victor. At least we have a few leads on the gunman," I said with my eyes averted downwards. I couldn't face my dear friend.

"Why Watson, you have it all backwards," my friend cheerily explained.

This startled me, and I actually made eye contact with Holmes who appeared quite jovial. "Whatever do you mean?" I inquired.

"All the information from Brigadier Victor I had already surmised on my own."

"You what? Holmes, that's astounding!" I admitted.

"It is actually rather elementary, my dear Watson. On the night of the assassination of Liddle, I noted that Rousseau and Bellows never mentioned reactions from the residents in the vicinity. A gunshot in the dead of night would have aroused at least some concerned citizens who would have investigated. The police officer on duty at Liddle's rooms would have been forced to answer questions as to why he was stationed there. The current officer is undercover, in civilian clothes, and to my knowledge, no one has made any inquiries as to the whereabouts of Liddle. When I went to his rooms and discovered them empty, I did a little investigating of my own at a local tavern. I pretended to be a new resident and mentioned to some that the area was rather noisy, that I had been awakened in the middle of the night by a loud bang. No one else there had heard anything, and a few grumbled that there were no quiet spots left in London, that the entire city was heading straight to Hades. Typical talk of those grumbling into an empty ale glass.

"With no one roused from their slumber by a rifle shot, I knew that meant the gun must have had some kind of silencing device. I did my own research into the matter and discovered that there are quite a few in existence, none patented yet, but it is only a matter of time."

I frowned. "So none of my pieces of information is useful to you."

"That is where you are wrong, Watson. Do you remember our conversation on the train ride to and from Sir Wellington's estate?"

"Of course, Holmes."

"And did you think I was speaking rather louder than was required?"

"Well, it was a rather noisy train …." I began.

"Yes, it was; however, I was talking well over the din of the locomotive and the passengers. For, I already knew that the droopy-eyed fellow was following us."

"This is astounding."

"I had noted the fellow following me earlier that day when I inspected Liddle's studio. At the time, he was disguised as a chair mender. He had on a shorter fake beard, and I instantly recognized the man as one who has gone incognito, and I must say that I was disappointed in his skills. With his loosely attached beards and poorly applied hair dyes, he would never last a moment on a London stage."

"If you recognized the man as being involved in the murder of Liddle, why did you not have a constable arrest him on the spot?"

"For the same reason that you were tailing the fellow, to learn what he knew. Was he the assassin? It was possible. Because he had no skills in espionage did not mean he had no skills in firing a weapon. Could he have been the forger of the Mycroft letter? Certainly not. Anyone with the brains and skills to complete such an authentic forgery would never resort to such obvious charades to gain information on me; no, that man would be certain that his craft was so well executed that he would have no fears of ever being arrested. This confirmed my suspicion that there was a group involved in this tangled web of theft, forgery, and murder.

"The people involved in the forgery crime were a separate lot from those who executed Mr Liddle," concluded Holmes.

"I don't understand," I admitted.

"Let me explain myself, Watson. Let us say that you were going to rob the Bank of England. You were one of the inside men, sometimes just a man but often two or three individuals, who worked in the bank. Your job was to make certain that the entryway to the bank vault was clear, that through an error in scheduling, no guard was on duty for a few hours that night. You also may be the one who makes sure the books show no sign of a reduction in the bank's holdings.

"Separate from you are the lower level criminals, those that work the streets of London. They break into the vault, steal £100,000, and disappear into the streets with their booty. The inside man and the common criminals know of each other's roles; however, they do not have any knowledge of who the other person is. If one group gets caught, often the other group goes free. I have found there are two ways to catch these criminals. One way is through their mistakes. A hidden ledger is discovered or some of the missing money turns up and leads a path to the crooks. The other way is from a mistake in the faith of the crime. Some criminals keep returning to the scene of the crime, double checking to ensure they are not caught. These sloppy criminals often lead us right back to their lair, and we arrest the lot of them."

"What does this have to do with you speaking loudly on the train?"

"I was getting the droopy-eyed fellow's attention. You may not have noticed, but he was with us the entire train ride to Belgravia, and he joined us as we switched trains at Piccadilly on our way back to Baker Street. I wanted this eavesdropper to know that we were aware of Liddle's Secret Service letter, that we had deduced it was a fake, and that we were going to see Sir Wellington. On the way home, I added in the details of learning something from discovering Liddle's room wiped clean. I wanted this man to get a little jumpy, and to keep following me, which he did on my first trip to the Portrait Gallery. What I did not expect was for him to switch targets today and follow you. From what you've told me, I believe he was ordered to do so."

THE ADVENTURE OF THE PECULIAR PROVENANCE

"Ordered? You mean he is not acting as a lone wolf, here. From what you were saying, I assumed he was nervous, unsure of himself, and would make a mistake which would lead you and the Yard back to his den of criminals."

"That is because that makes logical sense Watson. I was supposed to believe that line of reasoning, myself, and perhaps I would have as the dots connected and the modus ponens showed that A equalled C."

I scratched my head. "Holmes, you confuse me. You say you use logic but speak in riddles."

"Not intentionally, Watson," Holmes smiled. "I merely am saying that the person, or persons, behind this wanted me to believe that this droopy-eyed fellow would lead us back to them. In reality, he probably would have either purposely misled us or led me into a trap. But he made quite a faux pas when he stated that he was not to cause me harm."

"Will that assist you in solving the case?"

"My Dear Watson, I believe that, because of your information, the case is as good as closed."

"You mean you've solved it! But how, man?" I asked. My mind was reeling from our conversation.

"I am going to keep my tongue still for the moment, Watson. I need to double-check a few of my facts; however, I believe this case will be resolved to the satisfaction of Rousseau and the Yard by noon on Friday. You remember what I say about Chess?"

"That those who play the game have a scheming mind?"

"Yes, and I believe we are playing a game with a very skilled player. The pieces are on the board, and like a tournament champion, I believe I have seen my opponent's next four moves. The game will end in checkmate."

"Again, Holmes, you do not speak in plain English."

"And again, my dear Watson, I apologize. Now, I believe the ladies will be in the kitchen for at least another hour, so that gives me time to tell you of my activities today."

"Have you learned much?"

"Indeed I have," Holmes laughed. "I've learned that I'm the biggest fool in all of London."

Chapter 13

"Holmes, you know that you are the smartest man in all of London. How can you call yourself a fool?" I asked, feeling perturbed. "Are you playing games with me?"

"Watson, have you ever known me to play games?" Holmes asked, coldly.

"No, I suppose not, but to call yourself a fool is unheard of."

"And I insist," Holmes responded, now back to his jovial tone of voice, "that I am a fool. The solution to the problem of the peculiar provenance was right before me, and I didn't see it. Sometimes a complex mind, like mine, can make the complex quite simple, but it may also make the simple far too complex."

"Out with it, man! What happened?"

Holmes gave a silent laugh, then added more shag to his pipe before he began. "Last night, I went back over my notes, trying to ascertain how to get a break in this case. I thought of returning to see Sir Wellington to ask him more questions to see if he might provide another lead. Then, I thought of going to another museum and inspecting the provenance of some of their works of art. I thought, since I was focused on the Portrait Gallery, they may be more careful there, but not so much so in some of London's other museums and galleries. Then, the solution dawned on me. It was so obvious I actually called aloud a 'Ho-Ho!' That's when I realized I was a fool."

"If you are a fool then so am I. I still don't understand," I admitted.

Holmes raised his left hand and motioned me to be silent so that he could continue his tale, uninterrupted. "This morning, I again returned to the Bethnal Green Museum. This time, I did not wear a disguise, for I realized that was my main mistake before. If I had not been so dense then I could have solved this mystery at least a day earlier. When I entered the museum, I went straight to the office of Mr Melvin Gregory. I found the man to be as described by Sir Wellington. He is a rather nervous man who is thin and balding. When he met me, his eyes shifted about, and his shoulders hunched up. He had a hard time focusing on me, and I could tell he was dreadfully worried.

"'Do you know who I am?' I asked in a demanding voice.

"'N-no, sir,' Mr Gregory responded. His arms were clasped around his body, and he kept his eyes averted towards the ground.

"'I am Sherlock Holmes.' At the sound of my name, Gregory made eye contact. He looked up at me, his eyes full of awe.

"'Oh, Mr Holmes. You don't look a thing like your brother. Not at all. So sorry I didn't recognize you. So sorry,' Gregory apologized for something that did not require an apology.

"'No need for that,' I assured him. 'Please, may we speak in your office? My brother has sent me.'

"Gregory led me to his office, and in the confines of the room, he told me everything about the forgery.

"'Several months ago, Christmas Eve to be exact,' Gregory explained in a tremulous tone of voice. 'I was greeted by two tall men outside of the entrance to the museum. The two men were broad in the shoulder and had short, cropped hair. They looked like military men. They told me that they were members of the Royal Guard and that they had official orders to escort me to meet with an agent of the government.'

"'I asked where they were escorting me and under whose orders. It was Christmas Eve, after all, and I wanted to get home to my family for dinner before heading to church.

"'Under orders from her majesty, the Queen,' they informed me. 'You will see the location soon enough.'

"'I know enough not to question an order from the Queen, so I agreed to go with the gentlemen in their white carriage. The interior of the carriage was rather ornate, and the two stunning cob horses pulling us along told me that these gentlemen were legitimate servants of the Queen. I wondered what service I could supply her majesty. I was, after all, only a humble historian.

"'As we moved along the streets of London, I noted we were moving further and further East, away from Buckingham Palace, and I wasn't sure where we were going, but it did strike me as odd that the Queen would have official business far from the London crowds.

"'Eventually, the carriage stopped before a small cottage on the outskirts of the city, in the country really, and I was brought inside to find two additional guards and a rather large man sitting at a rather small oak table.'

Here, Holmes paused in his retelling of Gregory's incredible story. He took a few more puffs from his pipe, let the ethereal smoke bob and dance before dissipating in the air before him.

"Watson, I suppose you know who that rather large fellow was."

"Why, Holmes, was it Mycroft?" I asked my friend.

"Supposedly, it was. However, as Gregory described my brother, I knew it was a man in disguise. This supposed Mycroft always kept his face in shadow, and the fact that Gregory stated my brother and I have no family resemblance is a clear sign that the man was an imposter. Even though Mycroft and I have dissimilar body shapes, our faces are clearly from the Holmes family.

"Anyway, Gregory explained that he was told a very similar story as he told to Sir Wellington, that the Royal Family was in trouble, that they needed to raise funds to help the Portrait Gallery, and that the Royal Family was in dire need of additional funds as well. It was his duty to assist in this scheme.

"Gregory's role was to be that of the broker. He explained to me that he would be given the fake provenance for the portrait and that an artist would create the actual charcoal drawing. Gregory would then insert the provenance into the Gallery without anyone's knowledge, contact Sir Wellington, sell the drawing, and then hand over the payment to one of the guardsmen. Once the payment was received, Gregory would remove his false provenance and destroy it. No one would have a trail to follow to point to his deception. Even if Sir Wellington, or another duped individual complained, there would be no evidence, no witnesses, to indicate that the sale took place.

"'I made certain that your brother really was working in the interest of the Queen,' Gregory had told me, and he removed from his desk drawer an identical letter as the one that Liddle had in his possession. 'When I saw the official seal and your brother's signature, then I knew that the assignment was genuine. As a humble servant, what could I do but accept the task before me, even if I felt it was of a dubious nature.'"

"Once Gregory completed the deal, he waited one day. Then, one of the guardsmen who had escorted him to the rendezvous point with my brother's doppelganger, arrived at his office door. Gregory handed the payment over to the guard who thanked the man for his effort in upholding the honour of the crown.

"After Gregory finished his story, I questioned him about the guardsmen, the supposed royal carriage, the route to the cottage, and the cottage itself. By the time I had finished my inquiries, I believed that I could find the cottage on my own. I thanked Gregory for his service to the Queen, left the museum, hired a cab, and was on my way to the cottage."

"Holmes, did you not tell Mr Gregory of his deception?"

"No, Watson, I decided that would do no good. The man was nervous enough as it was," Holmes chuckled. "I did not want to give him a heart attack."

Holmes' statement made me chuckle as well. Then I asked, "What of the cottage? Did you find it?"

"Indeed, I did," Holmes explained. "It was no more than a shabby little house in squalor and disarray. I found no furniture inside beyond the oak table and chairs. Like Liddle's room, the entire cottage had been cleaned. No clues remained. Even the dirt in front of the house had been raked over so as not to leave any clues as to the whereabouts of the carriage."

"Holmes, it sounds like these villains are very good at covering their tracks. You have learned nothing more than that Gregory was a pawn in a treacherous scheme."

"Actually, I learned much more than that, Watson, though now you understand why I called myself a fool. Had I just gone straight to Mr Gregory dressed as I am now, admitting who I am instead of pretending to be a prominent art dealer, I would have saved myself a lot of time and may have kept you out of trouble. Once the man knew I was Sherlock Holmes, the brother of Mycroft, he told me all I needed to know."

I told my dear friend not to blame himself, and internally, I was happy to hear Holmes admit he had made a mistake which he saw as a rather simple one. "Besides being the fool that you are," I said, now speaking jovially myself. "What else did you uncover?"

Here, Holmes held up one of the forged Mycroft letters. "I made inquiries this afternoon at a few galleries and found no less than three additional people who were duped into this scheme. They, too, were brought to this cottage in the woods and were hired by my supposed brother. One of the three had completed his assignment, but two others were awaiting their fake artwork's arrival. I believe with the death of Liddle and by my investigation of the case, the villains have ceased their plans to continue on with more forgeries. We have stopped a rather lucrative scheme for these villains. Soon, the case will be officially solved, and Rousseau will be pleased."

"I still don't see how you will catch the crooks. It appears that they have all but disappeared into the ether."

"Not completely, my dear Watson. These thieves have shown a scheming mind, but also a proud one. Look for an article in *The Times* tomorrow on the current state of crime in London, and then prepare to join me on Friday morning at Scotland Yard. You will understand more then. Now, I believe I hear the ladies approaching. It is time for a respite from the crimes of London to enjoy a palatable feast."

Chapter 14

Mary and Martha supplied a delightful feast. We spent the evening discussing the pros and cons of gas versus coal stoves. Martha was still uncertain of removing her coal fuelled oven for fear that the gas stove would leave an unpleasant aftertaste to the food. With Mary's culinary skills, she proved to Mrs Hudson that the miracles of modern technology were far superior to that of our ancestors. Holmes even noted that soon we would have electric stoves, to which Martha replied, "One step at a time, Mr Holmes. I have not yet made up my mind on installing a gas stove. You already have me advancing into the twentieth century."

We all had a jolly good time and when Mary and I bade the detective and his landlady adieu for the night, we were all in high spirits. That evening I slept well, and when I awoke the next day, I was reminded of my assault by the sheer pain I felt around my gut. I rose from my bed and went through a few stretching motions to loosen up the muscles around that region of my body. I cursed my fortune and wished to be in my twenties again. I took my fair share of battering during my days playing Rugby, but none ever left me feeling like this.

Despite my pain, which was considerable, I forced myself down the stairs to have a breakfast before heading out to work and returning to my patients. When I arrived in the dining room, my sweet Mary had already gone out for the day, but she left me a breakfast of hardboiled eggs, mushrooms, tomato juice, and also the morning edition of *The Times*.

As I ate my breakfast, I read of the decision to hold the World's Fair in the American city of Chicago, and of the adventures of Henry M. Stanley in the wilds of Africa. I read of new construction in Manchester, and of the continuation of cold and blustery weather throughout Britain. I was alarmed, though, when my eyes scanned a brief article by Cecil Cummings, a reporter of dubious character, who never seemed certain of the difference between fact and opinion. Often, his articles focused on the gossip of London. He liked to focus on the mischief of those in society's upper crust, doing more insinuating with innuendo than ever proving anything beyond rumour. This morning, he had a brief article on the bungling criminals of London.

The Inept State of the Criminal Mind in London
By Cecil Cummings
The effort which is being made by certain men of unlawful character to commit acts of heinous crimes is surprisingly laughable. On Monday evening of this week, a burglar entered the residence of one Sir Hardwick Wellington of Belgrave Square. The criminal, a man who is currently in custody with Scotland Yard, attempted to abscond with a rare charcoal drawing of the great King Edward III. This criminal was so poor in his skills that after removing the portrait from the wall of Sir Wellington's study, he apparently stumbled over his own two feet and dropped the portrait into the study's fireplace. As fortune would have it, the portrait received minimal damage as only one edge of the drawing

was singed. The portrait was saved by Sir Wellington himself, and the thief left the premises empty handed.

Later that evening, the criminal was arrested by that most righteous of men, Chief Inspector Rousseau, who had no difficulty tracking the bumbling thief who in no way tried to hide his identity as he scurried about the streets of London in returning to his home. The criminal, probably in an inane escape attempt, somehow injured himself most severely before being brought to Scotland Yard. However, Chief Inspector Rousseau assures us that the criminal has recovered from his wounds and will face his trial tomorrow morning before the local magistrate.

It should be a fun time in the courtroom tomorrow as the burglar explains his moronic actions. Perhaps, he will tell the court if there were other clowns, or should I say crooks, involved in this comical caper. I have heard from reputable sources that the damaged portrait of King Edward III is currently being restored to its proper glory. Rumour has it that the image will be officially unveiled at the opening of the new National Portrait Gallery.

My cheeks glowed as I burst out laughing when reading this article for it dawned on me that Cecil Cummings was no more than a nom de plume for none other than Sherlock Holmes. Now, I knew what my friend was up to. Since these criminals had huge egos, nothing works better at drawing out those who are proud than to insult them.

I wrote my dear friend a letter explaining how brilliant I thought his plan was and told him I'd be at the Yard the following morning with my Webley, ready to assist the detective and the constables in any way I could.

THE ADVENTURE OF THE PECULIAR PROVENANCE

*

The next day, I arrived at the Yard bright and early. There was much bustling about, as constables and officers of the law walked back and forth, delivering messages, preparing to make rounds, or checking on prisoners. I found Holmes and Rousseau huddled together in front of the cell which contained Bellows pretending to be Liddle. I greeted the men warmly and they expressed their gratitude at my arrival and assistance.

"It is good to see you, Watson," Rousseau and Holmes said together. Bellows also was standing by the door to his cell. Colour had returned to his face, and he simply nodded at seeing me.

"Gentlemen, it is good to see you as well. What is our plan of action this morning? I expected to see more officers assisting in the transport of Bellows," I admitted. This was going to be a dangerous mission. We would need as much support as could be obtained.

"Everything is going according to plan, my dear Watson. We don't want to attract too much attention, but we have a number of undercover officers along the transport route. We will leave here with Liddle in a police wagon. Most likely the assailants will strike when we reach the Magistrate's Court. There is less of a police presence at the court than there is here at the Yard. It is also possible that they will strike at the prisoner while he is en route to his destination, though it is less likely as he will be secured inside the wagon. Still, it is a possibility.

"What is to be my role, Holmes?" I asked.

"You and I will ride next to the driver of the wagon. We will be disguised in uniforms. If we are attacked, we will be able to quickly move to safety. If we see anything suspicious, we will let out a loud whistle which will alert the constables hidden along the route. They will move in to arrest the assailant or assailants."

"Hmm," I pondered. "The plan is reasonable, as long as they actually strike."

"They will, Watson," Holmes assured me. "They will not resist an opportunity to kill Liddle and restore their honour."

*

All was made ready. Liddle was interned in the back of a police wagon. Holmes and I wore constable uniforms, plus a little something extra Holmes concocted. "I have something that will ensure your safety which I am requiring you to wear under your uniform," Holmes explained, and he showed me what appeared to be a chest and back plate of armour. "Don't give me that look, Watson. You know I made you promise just two days ago not to put yourself in harm's way, yet here I am asking you to risk your life. These plates of metal will strap in below your clothes. Once you have them on, if a bullet were to hit you in the front or back, it would stop it from killing you."

I thought of saying an impolite rejoinder, but I acquiesced. Holmes was right, I needed to take extra precautions for Mary's sake. Once I was wearing both of my outfits, I climbed aboard the wagon with Holmes and Babcock, a driver I had not had the pleasure of meeting before. He was a strong lad from Manchester who was a recent import to London.

THE ADVENTURE OF THE PECULIAR PROVENANCE

"Are you ready, Dr Watson," Babcock asked.

"I am, my good man. Are you?"

"Why, sitting here snug between Sherlock Holmes and Dr Watson, I feel like I'm in the safest place in the world."

I let out a hardy laugh at the driver's response, but Holmes responded, darkly, "You are driving into a dangerous situation. Do not take this assignment lightly. At the first sign of trouble, Watson and I will leap from the carriage, but the minute our feet hit the ground, you whip those horses and get them moving as fast as you can. Your life, indeed all of our lives, may depend on it."

We moved out on Whitehall at a steady pace. I kept my eyes upwards, staring at the tops of the buildings in our surroundings. The streets were bustling and buildings were active, but I saw no suspicious activity. At one point I saw what I thought was a man on a building roof, but he backed away from the edge, and I gathered it was one of the Yard's undercover agents keeping watch over us.

When we were a few blocks from our destination, I was beginning to think, perhaps, that Holmes was correct, in that the criminals would not strike until we were in front of the court building. Then I changed my mind and wondered if that would be a huge blunder on their part. Attacking at either Scotland Yard or at a court room seemed suicidal. There would be too many constables present. Then, I wondered if Holmes may have been completely wrong in how his opponents would react to the transport of Liddle. Perhaps he had underestimated these criminals, and perhaps they were more cautious than he gave them credit for. Maybe they even knew that Liddle was dead and that the portrait of King

Edward III was nothing more than a pile of ash. There were too many variables at play for even Holmes to be certain of how the crooks would act.

There was also the possibility that they had not seen the article Holmes had published under his alias in *The Times*. I thought I'd have to ask Holmes how he was able to write fake articles for the newspaper. Was this another favour of his brother, giving Holmes access to the press, or did his editor have no idea that Cecil Cummings was in reality a consulting detective? How many other identities, I wondered, did Holmes have? The man appeared to always have his eyes on every aspect of London.

As I pondered over the various identities of Holmes, I kept scanning the roof tops and upper level windows of the buildings we passed. Out of the corner of my eye, I noted a slow movement on the roof of a shoe factory we were approaching. At first, I thought it was another undercover officer, but then I noticed a long tube slowly extend over the edge of the roof. "Holmes!" I called out the moment my mind registered that I was staring at the barrel of a shot gun. Babcock stopped the coach for just a second as Holmes and I jumped to the ground. "Go, lad!" I shouted.

With a crack of the whips and a "Haw!" Babcock took off as fast as his horses could go, barrelling down the street and out of harm's way. The second the carriage bolted, we heard a series of three quick gunshots. Holmes and I dashed to the entryway of the factory building, out of the line of fire. We heard a fourth gunshot, a much louder one, and then there was silence. Holmes gave his signal whistle, though no officer of the law could have missed the echoing sounds of the gunshots.

"Quickly Watson!" Holmes said, and we burst inside the building, my nostrils hit by the fumes of leather and rubber. The noise of the factory was loud, and the workers continued on their jobs of assembling boots and shoes without giving us any notice. They had no way of hearing the gunshots over the steady hum of the factory.

Holmes and I barrelled up the factory steps to the roof. When we got to the access door, Holmes stopped and turned to me. "Are you ready, Watson? We could be moving into danger. I'm not sure what will greet us beyond this door."

I removed my Webley from my coat pocket. "I am ready, as always, old man," I said and readied for the plunge into combat. On a count of three, we slammed into the access door, opening it up, and charging out into the light of day. I expected to hear more gunshots or to be met by a group of assailants. I did not expect the sight which my eyes saw when they adjusted to the glow from the rays of the sun.

On the rooftop were two figures. The first was a constable, standing just outside the doorway, with a smoking pistol in his hand. The other was the shooter, slumped over the side of the building, clearly the victim of the officer's bullet.

Holmes approached the young officer. He was a green one, barely old enough to be on the force. Holmes put his left hand on the lad's shoulder and asked if he was all right.

"He didn't give me a choice," the officer admitted. "He turned and was going to shoot me. I had to…"

"You did right, constable," Holmes assured the officer. "My name is Sherlock Holmes and this is my associate Dr Watson."

"I know who you are, sir. There's not a constable at the Yard who doesn't know you, Mr Holmes."

Holmes nodded and asked the constable what happened.

"I was stationed to keep watch in this factory. I had ascended to the roof, when I knew the wagon with Liddle was approaching, and made certain it was all clear. I then went down to the top floor and made my rounds. Nothing seemed suspicious, when suddenly, a burly worker ran up to me and told me he saw a man with a rifle moving towards the roof. I ran upwards as fast as my legs could carry me, and before I opened the door, I heard three shots from the rifle. I opened the door to the roof and saw the gunman in position. I called to him, and he turned towards me, rifle in hand. I knew he'd shoot me if I gave him the chance, and so I fired, killing the man. I did right, didn't I, Mr Holmes?" The young constable asked, unsure of himself.

"I will see that Chief Inspector Rousseau commends you for your actions. You are a brave lad Constable-"

"Wiggins, sir. Constable Wiggins."

"Ah," Holmes smiled. "That seems to be the name of many a brave lad. I believe I hear more officers approaching, constable. They, too, will need to hear your story of bravery. With your permission, I'd like to inspect the body of the assailant with Dr Watson."

"Of course," Wiggins said proudly. "You don't need to ask my permission, Mr Holmes."

Holmes and I walked over to the body of the shooter. He was slumped over the edge of the building, and when I rolled him over to see his identity, I was greeted by the face of the droopy-eyed man who tried to kill me just two days before.

"It is the villain who accosted me, Holmes!" I snapped.

"As I expected," Holmes admitted. "I think you will also find that the remaining bullets in the man's pockets are blanks, that Bellows was never in harm's way, nor were any of us today."

"I don't understand, Holmes."

"This deceased assailant, though we have come to know him quite well, we still know very little about him. We have no name, no identifying papers. There is nothing in my records on this assassin. He was set up to take the fall, here. This, my friend, is a message."

"What type of message is this?" I asked coldly. A man was dead. What purpose did it serve?

"It is a message that the game is being played. This was the only loose thread of the crime syndicate which made a considerable amount of money duping wealthy people into buying imitation artwork. It is a sign that the scheme is over. You had identified this man, Watson. He had blundered when he revealed that he meant me no harm. He had to be removed before he blundered again and brought down his entire criminal network. The villains involved will move on to other means of income; indeed, I'm sure they currently have other lucrative revenue streams that work around the law."

"Then we have failed, Holmes."

"On the contrary, Watson. All has played out precisely as I anticipated."

"A man is dead Holmes. Thousands, maybe millions of pounds have been stolen from people buying worthless, fake art. We've arrested no one. How can you say that this has played out as expected?"

"Because, my dear Watson, this is a case which will take time. Some cases we solve neatly. Those are the cases you have scribed so well in *Beeton's* and *Lippincott's*. But other cases do not untangle so easily into a single narrative. This is a much larger criminal enterprise we face Watson. But they fell for my trap. They read the news article and responded by setting up this poor chap to take the fall. They do have high opinions of themselves, and I did bruise their egos. It would have been much safer for them to just kill this man in private and dump his body into the Thames. Instead, they wanted to make a point, to say that they are not the imbeciles portrayed in Cecil Cummings' news article."

"But why do they intend you no harm?" I asked.

"It is all part of the game they play. They see me as a worthy opponent, and until they tire of me, I will get a reprieve. Again, an error on their part. These gentlemen have an arrogance, and that can be exploited. It may take one year, it may take two, but I will catch these criminals in my web, Watson. I swear it."

"I assure you, Holmes," I said to my partner. "I will be by your side when you do."

*

When Rousseau arrived on the rooftop and saw that the shooter was the man who had attacked me, he was quite pleased. "We have our man," Rousseau explained to Holmes and me. "This case is now closed. I believe that Liddle and this shooter were a team. They planned on stealing Sir Wellington's portrait and then selling it to make a few thousand pounds. Liddle forged that letter from your brother, Mycroft, himself. He used it to try and trick us into letting him go. It didn't work though. I saw past that little charade.

"Then, when this droopy-eyed fellow saw that his friend had been arrested, he shot the man, and escaped," Rousseau concluded. He paused for a moment to give directions to a few constables who were inspecting the shooter's body.

"Thank you, Mr Holmes," Rousseau continued. "It was brilliance on your part for us to pretend that Liddle was still alive. It was also brilliant of you to send that information to Mr Cummings to write in that news article. It drew this crook out into the light. Funny fellow. Had he left you alone, Dr Watson, had he just run away after murdering his comrade, we never would have caught him."

Holmes had been correct. The case was closed to the satisfaction of Chief Inspector Rousseau. In his mind, he had connected the dots in a way that constructed a narrative which left him, and now also Constable Wiggins, taking the credit for the death of a dangerous man. He believed he had done his duty in keeping London safe. If only he knew of the dangerous minds working below the facade of London pleasantry.

Chapter 15

The following morning, I ventured to Baker Street, to return the tin Mrs Hudson had used to transport her delicious cornucopias to my house, for our dinner party. When I saw Martha, she looked much more relieved than the last time I saw her. Her shoulders were relaxed and a mood of cheeriness had returned to her.

"Please let Mary know I cannot thank her enough for inviting me to your home for dinner," Mrs Hudson explained. "I very much enjoyed the evening out, and Mary convinced me that it was time to purchase a gas fuelled stove. It may cost me a bit now, but I think I will earn every shilling back in the time it will save me."

I agreed and assured Mrs Hudson that Mary would send another invitation soon, but this time it would be for a gathering of just women.

"I look forward to it, Dr Watson. Don't get me wrong. It is always a pleasure to see you, but sometimes, we hens need time to ourselves."

With a chuckle, I heartily agreed and then ascended the stairs to see Holmes. I was happily surprised to find not one Holmes, but two. The brothers were sitting together on the sofa, chatting, with Mycroft taking up two cushions while Sherlock's thin form barely took up half of one.

"Gentlemen," I said on entering the room. "I hope I am not interrupting you."

"Not at all," Holmes said. "We were just reminiscing about one of my former tutors who used to work with me back at Holmes Hall. We believe we will see more of that gentleman in the future. Now, Watson, what brings you here?"

"Just running an errand for Mary, returning a cookie tin," I explained, though my mind wondered why the Holmes brothers were discussing a tutor. Holmes never reminisced about his childhood. I put speculation out of my mind and turned to Mycroft. "It is good to see you, Mycroft. I thought you were not yet due to return from France."

"You remember correctly, doctor. I was to return tomorrow; however, when I received the message from Sherlock, I decided it would be best to return in a timelier fashion."

"You have informed Mycroft of everything?" I asked and took a seat in my favourite chair.

"Yes, he is now caught up, and Watson, you are just in time to see the end to the final loose thread of this caper."

I was uncertain of what Holmes meant, but I did detect a loud clopping on the stairs and the sound of Mrs Hudson's voice with that of a gentleman.

Soon, Martha entered and announced Sir Hardwick Wellington. Holmes called the man in, and Sir Wellington clomped his way into the room, using his wolf-headed cane for support. Also, his servant, Ronald entered as well, his corpulent form barely squeezing through the doorway.

I could tell Wellington was surprised to see all three of us in the room, his ichthyic eyes getting even wider, and a malicious grin appeared on his face when he saw Mycroft, was introduced, and discovered that Mycroft worked for the British government. "Mycroft Holmes," Sir Wellington said with a slight guttural chuckle. "It is good that you are here. I assume your brother has told you everything about my case."

"He has, Sir Wellington," Mycroft agreed, and I swear that Wellington greedily licked his lips, like a witch from one of the Grimm Brothers' tales.

"Before we continue, Sir Wellington, there is an issue of my payment," Holmes said, sternly. "As I know you have issued a claim to collect your insurance money on the destroyed King Edward III, the payment of £5,000 should be readily available."

Sir Wellington let out one of his odd growls that sounded like a primal beast. "The money is not as readily available as you would think," Wellington admitted, but he removed his cheque book from his pocket, and at Holmes' invitation took a seat at his desk and began filling out a cheque. "That daft fool Cummings who wrote the article in *The Times* a few days ago, made it seem like the portrait was only singed in the fire. I now have to deal with insurance agents questioning my honesty and integrity. Still, that has nothing to do with you, Mr Holmes."

As Wellington finished writing out the cheque, I looked over at his servant Ronald who stood quietly by the door. I wondered if he and Mycroft sat on the sofa together if the furniture would snap from the sheer weight of the gentlemen.

Wellington stood from the desk and handed the cheque over to Holmes who folded it up and put it in his pocket. "You will have nothing to fear, Sir Wellington. That article was written by a man who does not know the difference between fact and opinion. I believe you will have your insurance money in the very near future."

THE ADVENTURE OF THE PECULIAR PROVENANCE

"Are you all right, Dr Watson?" Wellington asked.

I had to cough into my hands to cover for the fact that I was laughing aloud. I could not believe how masterfully Holmes had insulted himself, yet I was the only one in on the joke. Well, perhaps Mycroft was also in on the joke, but it is unlike Mycroft to so much as smile, let alone chuckle. "I am fine," I assured Sir Wellington, "just a bit of a cough."

"Now," Sir Wellington began, addressing Mycroft. "Has everyone been informed of my deceit by Mr Gregory?"

"Yes, I have notified the Board of the National Portrait Gallery as well as high level servants of the Royal Family."

"Good, good, that is all I needed to hear. Thank you Mr Holmes and Mr Holmes. Heh-heh, I guess there are two of you here. You have done a great service to your country. Has Gregory been arrested yet?"

"Why no," said Sherlock Holmes. "On the contrary, he is going to be commended."

"Commended?" Sir Wellington questioned, then he burst out laughing. "Surely, you jest."

"I assure you that I do not jest, not at all. Mr Gregory has shown himself to be a most humble and obedient servant to the Queen. He has assisted the Yard in discovering other forged works of art, and he has proven himself fully dedicated to The National Portrait Gallery. From what Mycroft tells me, the man will be promoted."

"Ridiculous!" howled Sir Wellington. "That man is a criminal! I have been wronged!"

"And how have you been wronged?" Holmes asked, coolly. "You have been tricked, that is true; however, you have filed a claim on your losses and will receive full compensation. I regret that I cannot explain more details due to issues of national security; however, I have made certain that the Board of the National Gallery also was informed of how you were tricked into purchasing the fake Edward III. They were most taken aback by how such a prominent art dealer from a noted family could be duped so easily."

Wellington shook with anger. "That is not how things were to turn out!" he raged.

"I am well aware of how you intended these events to turn out. You, Sir Hardwick Wellington, saw this as your opportunity to become employed by the National Portrait Gallery. You were hoping that the trick played upon you would lead to the termination of Mr Gregory, that a scandal would need to be silenced, that the way to silence the scandal would be to hire you as the new director of the gallery. You saw this as your opportunity to restore your family name. Instead, you have once again wounded your family's reputation."

Wellington lifted his walking stick up above his head, ready to strike at Holmes.

"You have no right to speak to Sir Wellington that way," Ronald scolded us. "He is a knighted member of the- OOWW! Master Wellington, please!" Wellington had looked to strike Holmes but instead he turned his weapon towards his servant, thrashing him with the cane.

"You dare speak without my permission!" Wellington scolded. "You dare!" After striking Ronald several times, Sir Wellington wobbled for a moment, and lowered the cane down to the ground, to assist in maintaining his balance. This only made Wellington more furious, and he spat upon the floor and screamed at all of us, "You men are fools! Do you hear me? Fools! You will rue this day, mark my words, I, Sir Hardwick Wellington, will have my revenge!"

With that, the grumbling man called to Ronald to follow, and they hurried down the stairs, Sir Wellington moving as fast as he could go on his three legs.

"A decidedly volatile, fellow," Mycroft quietly observed.

"Indeed, quite volatile," Holmes agreed. He then rose from the sofa and grabbed his hat and coat. "If you will excuse me for a moment gentlemen. I need to run to the bank to make a deposit before Sir Wellington cools down enough to remember he can still cancel my cheque. Do help yourselves to some brandy. I will return shortly."

With that Holmes said a quick goodbye and hurried down the stairs.

DERRICK BELANGER

Afterword

As is stated in the opening of this adventure, Dr Watson never intended anyone beyond Mr Adams from reading this story; however, since over 100 years have passed, the estate of Dr Watson saw no harm in the publishing of this adventure. In fact, it is believed that the additional pieces of forged artwork mentioned in this tale either were destroyed in one of the two World Wars or had been discovered as fakes in the proceeding decades.

I would like to thank my dear friends, the Adams family, for allowing me access to the Watson letters. It has been difficult taking letters between two individuals and turning them into a story written in the style of Dr Watson, but I feel it is the best way to reveal these stories. Please excuse any faux pas on my part. I have done my best to write in the Anglican English of Dr Watson as well as using the language of the time period. If any errors have occurred, the mistakes are on my part, and not that of the dear doctor.

Through reading over the letters, I have discovered a much clearer picture of the notorious Professor Moriarty, mentioned briefly in this story by Holmes as his childhood tutor. Future stories will flesh out the role Moriarty played in the crimes of London and throughout the world from 1890 to his demise at the Reichenbach Falls on May 4, 1891. There are also stories of Holmes and Watson coming to America in the early twentieth century as well as adventures between

THE ADVENTURE OF THE PECULIAR PROVENANCE

Holmes and Adams in the 1930s. I look forward to revealing more of these adventures as I continue to sort through the letters and untangle some rather intriguing narratives.

Sincerely,
Derrick Belanger

The Case of the Vanished Killer

DERRICK BELANGER

(Editor's Note: The following story was discovered fairly intact within a letter Dr Watson wrote to the young Archibald Adams. I consulted police reports and news articles of the time period to flesh out the story about the murder of the Smith siblings.)

It was a late Saturday morning on the first of October when I heard word of the double murder of the Smith siblings, a crime which held the attention of all of England for a few brief weeks in the waning months of 1887. Although the case is now well known throughout the Commonwealth, the role my friend played in solving the crime has been ignored and credit given to our own Scotland Yard. While England's brave officers deserve their fair share of credit for assistance on this adventure, I believe the murder would still be an unsolved crime, possibly one as famous and with as many outlandish theories as that of Jack the Ripper, if it weren't for Sherlock Holmes bringing the case to a swift conclusion.

The tale begins with me stirring bleary eyed in my bedroom at 221B Baker Street. My wife was overseas visiting her mother in Missouri, and I moved back in with Holmes for a few weeks to spend extra time with my dear friend. I had difficulty sleeping the previous evening as the weather was excessively chilly, and I awakened to find frost on my window and the sun already high in the morning sky. I joined Holmes in the dining room where he had already imbibed two cups of Darjeeling tea and completed the morning edition of *The Times*.

"Good morning, Watson," Holmes said while folding up the paper, "you have risen just in time for a breakfast certain to warm you on this frigid autumn day."

Mrs Hudson had prepared a fine meal of poached eggs on toast, grilled ham that was slightly crispy, and browned tomatoes. We drank orange juice with our breakfast and talked briefly about the recent cold spell which had enveloped all of England. This pleasant start to the day was interrupted by a ringing of the doorbell and Mrs Hudson delivering Holmes a note.

I could tell by Mrs Hudson's wide eyes and slight smile that this was no ordinary visitor.

Holmes looked at the note and handed it back to Mrs Hudson. "Well Watson," he stated, "it looks like we have a celebrity in our midst. Please, Mrs Hudson, show the gentleman in."

It did not take Holmes's powerful reasoning skills to know the identity of his guest. Mrs Hudson opened the door and a man in a rather dour black suit entered. Even out of costume, his notorious Van Dyke beard and long, flowing brown hair clasped back in a ponytail would leave any Londoner no doubt as to the gentleman's identity.

"Thank you for seeing me, Mr Holmes," the man started in a drawl only spoken by natives of the American West. He turned to me and offered his hand. "Hello, my name is-"

"Buffalo Bill Cody," I said rising from the table and meeting his hand in a firm grip. "Thank you, my name is Dr John Watson."

"Ah yes," Mr Cody said as we shook hands then released our grip. "Heard about you. You're the guy writing that novel about this fella dealing with those Mormons," he said referring to my forthcoming book, *A Study in Scarlet.*

"Let me assure you," Holmes responded, "that the actual solving of the case was not as dramatic as its portrayal in Dr Watson's telling. Now, please have a seat, and let us know what brings a famous entertainer such as yourself to my residence."

Mr Cody sat down in an easy chair, and we three pulled our chairs around in a circle. "First off, let me apologize for bothering you on the weekend. Know that I wouldn't be here if it weren't mighty important."

Holmes silently motioned with his wrist for Mr Cody to get to the point.

"Anyway, I need your help sir, very much sir. You see this Inspector Lestrade is threatening to keep my whole show from going on tonight. I can't afford to have a cancelled performance, but without my Indians, I'm not sure what to do."

At the mention of Lestrade, Holmes's ears perked up and the detective leaned forward clearly interested in the cowboy's tale.

"Mr Cody, before I can tell you if I can help you, I must know the details of why Inspector Lestrade, a man I can assure you I know quite well and a man I have, on many occasions, shown the error of his ways, is interested in keeping your Indians from performing."

"Well sir, did ya'll hear about the murder committed last night?"

"Murder," I said raising my eyebrows in surprise.

"Yes, Watson," Holmes calmly informed me. "It is the headline of this morning's *Times*. As usual, the article includes all the grisly details but none of the important aspects of the crime. Last night, or should I say, early this morning, a brother and sister with the last name of Smith were brutally murdered in their tenement building. The building is on Old Montague Street, in the Whitechapel district. There was no apparent sign of a break in. No money was stolen. The brother was found dead with a hatchet in his head, and the sister was found on the fourth floor landing, stabbed to death. At the time of the newspaper's publication, the police had no witnesses and no suspects. I assume that has changed."

"Right you are," answered Cody. "At just about dawn this morning, this Inspector Lestrade and half of Scotland Yard comes bursting into my Indians' sleeping quarters. They're hollering and screaming that one of my performers is guilty of killing these Smith siblings in cold blood. Fortunately, Red Shirt was there and was able to keep the peace. With all that hollering at six in the morning, after my troop had rightly stayed up late celebrating, we're lucky no fights broke out, and no one got arrested."

Red Shirt was the name of the famous Lakota-Sioux leader who was part of Bill Cody's Wild West show. The press loved the Indian and he was almost as famous as the cowboy before me. I was baffled as to why Mr Cody was telling us about how Inspector Lestrade connected the Indians to the murder and said as much to the gentleman.

"Well, apparently it wasn't no ordinary hatchet that killed that Smith boy. It was a tomahawk they found in his head,

THE CASE OF THE VANISHED KILLER

and that's not all. They also claim they found a few arrowheads on the floor of the apartment. That was what led the inspector to jump to the conclusion that an Indian had killed the Smiths. And, of course, where else to find an Indian but at my Wild West show."

Holmes leaned back in his chair for a moment, taking in the description of Mr Cody's situation. "Lestrade," the detective stated, "does have some rationale for his actions. Can you vouch for the location of all of your Lakota members?"

Mr Cody's spine stiffened, and I feared my friend had insulted the celebrity, but when he spoke his voice was quiet and serious. "Mr Holmes, I assure you that there ain't a one of my tribesmen who would commit such a crime. After last night's performance, as I said, they celebrated something fierce. I don't see how any of them would have had the capabilities to trek halfway across London, commit a murder, and return back to camp without anyone, including Red Chief, knowing they had gone missing."

"You admit there was a celebration that evening. In the general mood of celebrating, one could-"

"On my honour, sir!" Buffalo Bill interrupted my companion sternly, and he placed his right hand upon his heart. "On my honour, my men are innocent."

Holmes was silent for a moment. Then he nodded his head. "I cannot guarantee that my conclusion will satisfy you, nor that I will have solved the crime within your allotted time frame; however, I will be happy to provide my full attention to this matter."

The long haired cowboy gave a solemn nod of his head and the two men shook hands.

After bidding Mr Cody adieu, Holmes and I quickly dressed and hailed a cab. We moved swiftly through the streets of London from Baker to Old Montague. Holmes was quiet at the beginning of the ride, his elbows resting on his knees and his hands resting, palms together before his face, as if my friend were in a meditative prayer. I knew he was deep in thought, preparing himself for the case at hand.

"The details of the case," the detective suddenly began, "do have some points of interest, at least as far as their description in *The Times* and by that of Mr Cody. A brother and sister in a fourth floor apartment, murdered. The brother was killed with an axe; the sister with a throwing knife.

"The sister, a Miss Olivia Smith," Holmes continued, motioning me to be silent, "managed to stumble out into the hallway and call for help. As she lay dying, she pointed up the stairs, indicating that her accoster had escaped by ascending. The murderer fled to the roof, a seeming dead end, yet when some tenants climbed the stairs and searched the roof, they could find no trace of anyone. How does one ascend a set of stairs to the roof of a building and simply disappear?"

"Why, Holmes," I started, "it boggles the mind."

"Indeed," Holmes continued. "But we have not had a chance to visit the crime scene ourselves. My only hope is that ten hours after the crime was committed, the constables have left enough clues untrampled for my assistance to be of value. Aaahhh, Watson, we have arrived at our destination,"

THE CASE OF THE VANISHED KILLER

Holmes said as the coach came to a stop in front of a large tenement building. Holmes paid the cabbie and we were greeted by the constable out front. He ushered us into the building, and we climbed the stairs to a front room on the fourth floor.

Waiting outside the door was a bleary eyed sergeant, reflecting on his notes, and shifting his eyes nervously about. Two other constables were wandering around, making sure no residents approached the crime scene. When the sergeant saw Holmes, he stepped back in surprise. "Sherlock Holmes, so glad to see you!" the sergeant warmly greeted my friend. "Has Inspector Lestrade sent you?"

Holmes merely nodded. "Sergeant Rousseau, I understand you are having issues with finding a suspect for this case. While Inspector Lestrade is interviewing the Indians at Earl's Court, I have been asked to look into the crime and view the crime scene."

I had to hold back a chuckle as I noted that Holmes did not tell the sergeant who had asked him to investigate.

"It is a rather odd case, indeed," the white haired, sergeant started, and he scratched at his whiskery chin. "Usually my men and I can solve our own crimes, but there are parts to this case that are perplexing." The sergeant gave out a loud yawn and apologized. "I was covering for Constable Stevenson last night, and I was the first officer at the scene of the crime. With everyone running about now, I'm not sure when I will be relieved of my shift."

"Why not tell me the details, and I will do my best to assist you in whatever way I can," Holmes explained in a humble manner.

Sergeant Rousseau recounted the details Holmes had read in *The Times*, but he filled in many of the story's gaps. The gaunt faced man explained, "As I'm sure you know, we have had a terrible time keeping members of our force. I was covering for Constable Stevenson who has come down with a severe case of the flu. While walking the rounds, at approximately one a.m., I overheard cries of murder from a fourth floor window of the building in which we are standing. Upon my arrival, I found several residents cradling the dying form of Olivia Smith. After seeing that her wound was mortal, indeed, the life had already fled from the poor girl, I ascended the stairs in pursuit of the criminal. He was easy to track as I noted a trail of bloody footprints that continued along the stairwell to the roof. On the roof itself, a flat style, the footprints mysteriously vanished. There was no trace of the murderer. I searched every corner of the roof and noted the buildings and alleys surrounding the tenement. There was no movement that caught my eye, no sign of a fleeing suspect.

"I then returned to the Smith's front room," he said, motioning to the area he was currently guarding, "and discovered the body of Donald Smith, the younger brother of Olivia. His body was slumped over the sofa. At this point, more officers arrived at the crime scene, in response to the calls for help. The residents also were beginning to come out of their corners to see what all the fuss was about."

"I suppose you let them trample all over the stairs and the crime scene," Holmes stated sternly.

"The officers did their best to hold back the curious and helpful, to keep evidence from being disturbed. I think you'll find they did an exceptional job," Rousseau said coolly. He did not appreciate Holmes questioning his police work.

"A search of the apartment left no clue as to the motivation of the crime," Rousseau continued. "There were no missing jewels. A locked safe box was discovered and appeared undisturbed. There was no sign of a break in. The door to the living quarters was unlocked," Rousseau finished.

Holmes thanked Rousseau for his information. "I believe it is time for us to have our own look at the Smith residence, aye Watson," Holmes said to me, and then he whispered, "Despite Rousseau's assurances, let us hope the constabulary did not do too much damage to the crime scene."

Rousseau led us into the Smith's sparsely decorated lodging. The room consisted of a rather shabby, single bed; a sofa coated in the blood of Donald Smith; a central pine table, with a repaired, oak left side leg; a chiffonier adorned with family photos; and a small safe in the corner, with the door now open, yet, as Rousseau had reported, no valuables missing.

"Rousseau and I will inspect the room," Holmes instructed, "I'd like you to read over the autopsy report on the Smith siblings."

The detective and sergeant wandered about the room. Holmes lifted the family photos, checked the blood stains on the floor, and inspected the open safe. I read the report on The Smith siblings. Both had been murdered in a most grisly fashion. Olivia Smith had been mortally wounded with a stab to her chest. The knife entered deep, penetrated the thoracic cavity. A Pneumothorax developed causing both lungs to collapse. For Donald Smith, the hatchet had been deeply rooted in the skull and had pierced the brain, rendering death instantaneously. I looked down at the sofa which was coated in the man's blood, and I noted thick gobs that had dried upon the right sofa cushion, clearly indicating this is where the man's head had slumped when he died.

When Holmes joined my side, I could tell he had seen much more than the sergeant and his police force.

"Well Holmes and Dr Watson, have you learned anything that has escaped us?" asked Rousseau. I handed the detective the police report on Donald Smith, and he examined it closely, then responded. "We still have much more of the crime scene to investigate; however, I can assure you that Donald and Olivia were not brother and sister. They were lovers."

"Lovers?" Rousseau asked astonished.

"Yes, if you look closely at the family photos you will notice both Donald and Olivia Smith together, holding hands in some of the photographs. The family portrait of all the matriarchs of the family has Olivia's left hand slightly concealed behind her dress. Even so, the edge of a diamond ring is clearly visible. Lastly, while the bed is a single, clearly it has the impressions of two bodies. Yes, indeed Sergeant, the Smiths were not only lovers, they were husband and wife."

As my friend explained his reasoning, I could see the truth behind the words dawn upon Rousseau's face as his look went from one of astonishment to one of being dumbfounded. I sympathized with the sergeant as I had the exact same feeling, one I've had on many occasions with Mr Holmes.

THE CASE OF THE VANISHED KILLER

"That is truly astonishing, Mr Holmes. I'm not sure how we could have missed it. Does that have any bearing on the case?"

I awaited a sarcastic quip from Holmes, but he was in a serious state, and merely responded. "I'm not sure as of yet. Come Watson. I'd like your opinion of the bloody footprints."

As we left the Smith residence, I started seeing the faint outlines of the bloody prints. It was just the left foot, in fact just the tip of the left foot. I couldn't make out much more than the man had stepped in a bit of spilled blood which had remained on his foot. Holmes stopped on occasion and observed the footprints with his magnifying glass while Rousseau complained about the lack of officers on the force. Apparently, one constable sprained his ankle in all the rushing around the previous evening, leaving the Yard with one less patrolman. Eventually, we climbed onto the roof and were met with a burst of sunlight.

The roof was nondescript except for one fact. The buildings surrounding this tenement were several floors taller than the current one. An alleyway separated the building on the Northeast and Southeast sides from the next closest residences. Even if a thief could make the leap across the alleys on either side, they would surely smash into the brick walls of the neighbouring buildings. The Southwest side of the building was close to another tenement, though this one had an exceedingly steep thatched roof. For one to leap onto this roof and work one's way down to the ground seemed difficult. To do so without being observed, impossible.

"Our prey is a skilled devil," Rousseau cursed.

"These are dark dealings, sergeant," Holmes agreed. I notes that Holmes was looking at a scuff mark on the Northeast side of the building. What it could mean, I knew not, but I did notice a glimmer of recognition in my friend's eyes.

"It's a shame," Rousseau lamented. "If Lestrade isn't able to crack any of the savages at that circus then this case may never be solved."

Holmes glared at Rousseau, his mouth turning into a deep frown. "If, by savage, you mean an Anglo man of approximately five feet in height, of a particularly strong and limber body, who is undoubtedly from New York, and who was associated with the Smiths, then yes, I'd agree with you. As far as the Lakotas from Mr Cody's Wild West show are concerned, they are completely innocent."

After Holmes's tongue lashing of the sergeant, we made our way back out of the tenement building. "To me, this killer has done the impossible, yet you are onto something, aren't you?" I asked my friend.

"Remember, cases that seem impossible often have the simplest conclusions. I have noted four possible solutions to the case, but I still need more facts before I can deduce the resolution. For now, I need my Boswell's gift of observation."

"Whatever I may do to assist you, Holmes."

"There is a tavern there," said Holmes pointing to a dingy, dilapidated first floor establishment almost directly across the street. "I would like you to interview the barkeep and see if he had any notable customers yesterday evening. Take copious notes, and then send them to me when you are finished."

"Where will you be?" I asked.

"Why, at Earl's Court, attempting to show our dear friend Lestrade some semblance of reason."

I nodded and said goodbye to my friend. I expected him to hail a cab, but I was surprised to see Holmes instead enter the building neighbouring the Northeast side of the Smith's tenement.

The pub across the way had seen better days. The bar was stained different colours in several areas, crude attempts at covering up its missing chunks of wood. The furniture was a mix of different style tables and chairs from the last thirty years. The lighting was dark, the establishment drab, and the bloated barkeep with three shabby customers were the only people present. I noted that the customers kept their coat collars up and their heads face down in their ale. Not to stay hidden from me, but to stay hidden from the world. Such was the glum life of the alcoholic.

The barkeep, ruddy cheeked and with a crooked smile lit up when he saw me enter, possibly because of my dress and obvious station in life. I joined the rank group at the counter, ordered a pint, and struck up a casual conversation with the gentleman who introduced himself as Daniel Spitzer. It was my good fortune to discover the man was not only of jolly spirits but quite a talker. After discussing London's cold spell for a moment, I turned the conversation towards the Smith siblings.

"That's a terrible business, mind you, what with all that hullabaloo last night. Who would have thought that could happen to a nice couple like that?"

"Couple?" I inquired. "The *Times* said they were siblings."

"Oh, they claimed that they were brother and sister. Not sure why, not sure what they were fleeing from really, oh don't look surprised. If a couple is pretending to be siblings, you know that they are hiding from someone. It always puzzled me, but I never asked, though I've got an inkling as to what they were running from. You see, the death of the Smiths is terrible for them, but it's also terrible for me," he added with a wink.

"What do you mean terrible for you?"

"No shame telling you that the bar is only a portion of my income. A good chunk of my money also comes from the track, and the Smiths were some of my best clients. You see they bet big, but often lost just as big. I'm not sure where all their money came from, but between you and me, I bet they were swindlers. Nice folks here, always stayed out of trouble, but they had something about them, always looked a little haunted, if you ask me."

Mentioning the tracks and horses lead to a separate discussion on the prospects of the thoroughbred Ocean Breeze in the upcoming afternoon race. After placing a small wager with Spitzer, I turned the conversation back to the previous evening, and I was surprised to discover that he had been working during the time the crime was committed. "Yes, sir, I pretty much live here. I have to leave to go down to the tracks on occasion, but there isn't a day that goes by where I'm not here at least 14 hours. Anyway, last night, guess it would have been after one, people started flooding in. Some even had blood on their clothes. One poor officer looked stunned and shaken, same with two of the men, their clothes covered in blood. I'm guessing they were kicked out by the police before they had a chance to even change their clothes."

"Did you know the two men?" asked Watson.

"I know one of them, Abe Bruder, a jeweller near the Black Lion. Can't miss his flowing beard. Even that had streaks of blood in it. The man badgered on and on with a group of my people. Talked about holding the poor body of Miss Smith as she breathed her last breath. They were most upset, with good reason."

I pondered this information for a moment. Old Montague Street was known as having a predominantly Jewish population. I wondered if I would need to seek out a translator to assist with the Hebrew of the residents.

Finally, I pressed Spitzer again about anything else unusual that evening. He shrugged. "Nothing more than you'd expect. Lots of wailing and crying about the neighbourhood and our lot in life. No one struck me as standing out. Everyone was shaken from the murder."

I finished my ale and began to say goodbye when suddenly a thought occurred to me. "Do you know of any Americans who frequent your establishment?" I asked.

Daniel's eyes lit up. "Course I do, know of one man in particular who hails from New York. He's in here all the time."

I was surprised by this bit of good luck and asked for this man's name.

"Course you can have his name. You've been speaking to him for the better part of an hour," Daniel beamed.

Puzzled, I inquired what Daniel meant.

"It's me you fool. I'm originally from Buffalo, New York."

After my interview with Spitzer, I had my notes sent to Holmes, and returned to our residence. Relaxing, I enjoyed a glass of brandy and continued reading of Miss Nellie Bly's adventures in the book, *Ten Days in a Mad-House*, an appropriate title to reflect upon while sorting this case. Here was a girl voluntarily going undercover to expose the mistreatment of women in Blackwell's Island Asylum in New York. I wondered how many monsters lived in that American colony, and in my mind cursed our luck that Britain hadn't squashed General Washington's rebellion over a century ago. In due course, the brandy worked its effects, and I dozed off only to be awakened by Holmes shaking me a few hours later.

"Wake up, Watson," Holmes insisted. "We are to be guests at Mr Cody's Wild West Show this evening. Mrs Hudson is preparing a dinner of roast beef for us, and we should have just enough time to sup before our carriages arrive."

"Holmes, really," I started. "Do you have the solution to this dastardly case? Was it one of Mr Cody's Indians?"

"I almost certainly do have the solution, and I assure you Mr Cody's Indians had nothing to do with the crime."

"Well, out with it man," I demanded. "What happened?"

"You will accept my apologies Watson, as I cannot quite tell you the solution yet. There is still one last piece of the

THE CASE OF THE VANISHED KILLER

puzzle which I shall put in place tomorrow when one of Lestrade's men will join us. I believe he will identify the killer."

"But how?" I insisted. "How did the man pull this off?"

"In due time, Watson," Holmes answered coyly. "I believe you will find this evening's performance most enlightening. It took some convincing on my part, but once I assured Lestrade I'd have the murderer behind bars by tomorrow afternoon, he agreed to let Cody's show go on. Personally, I think the inspector just wanted an excuse to go home and finally catch up on much needed sleep."

*

After a delicious dinner of roasted beef and stewed vegetables, Holmes and I descended the stairs and waited for our coach to arrive. I was taken aback to see not one but three carriages stop in front of our home. Puzzled at why three carriages were needed for two men, I was about to ask Holmes when the answer came round the corner. Jostling towards us was a group of street urchins, dressed in dirty rags and making all sorts of noise as they tramped and jumped excitedly.

Holmes lit up at seeing the rag tag army marching towards us. "Hello, Thaddeus, hello Barney," he addressed two of the older boys in the front. "Is this everyone for the Wild West performance?"

"Yes, Mr Holmes," answered Thaddeus, a tall lad, thin, not from his body type but from his lack of nourishment. "There's a dozen of us, sir." He paused then quietly added in a tone of astonishment. "Golly, are we really gonna meet Mr Cody?"

"Of course you are, lad, as long as we make the show on time. Plus, Mr Cody has agreed to treat everyone to all the snacks they can eat."

A grand hurrah went up from the children, and then they scrambled into the growlers. I noted how one of the drivers scowled at seeing his passengers, but he kept his mouth shut, and with a crack of the reins, we were all off to the show. Holmes looked rather cheerful. "I wonder Watson, what will be more entertaining, seeing the show, or seeing the expressions of awe on the Irregulars' faces when they see the performances?" I heartily agreed, but inside I wondered what Buffalo Bill Cody would think of his rag tag special guests for the evening.

Fortunately, Mr Cody was as gracious and kind as the stories in the adventure books make him out to be. When we arrived at the fair ground, Cody was there to meet us, dressed in his stage costume, with his grey cowboy hat, tan shirt with fringe, dark riding boots, and his arms filled with a dozen bags of peanuts for the irregulars. After handing out food and shaking hands with the children, the showman led us to our seats. While the giddy children oohed and awed at the spectacle of the show grounds, Holmes asked Mr Cody, "Did you honour my request?"

"I sure did, Mr Holmes. Not exactly an authentic portrayal, but I doubt the audience will mind. I reckon you folks are in for one great show. Now, here are your seats. I best get ready."

After the showman had left, I asked Holmes about their side conversation. The detective was distracted, beaming with pride at seeing the boisterous excitement of the irregulars.

"It is tragic Watson, that my investigative team of children so rarely get to act like children," Holmes lamented.

The irregulars always left me a bit unsettled. The unsupervised children had a wild edge about them, but I conceded that Holmes was correct. It was nice to see all of them excited about a spectacle, not about a morsel of food to alleviate their growling stomachs.

"As to your question, Watson, I asked Mr Cody to add an act to tonight's performance that I had the pleasure of viewing during rehearsals this afternoon. I believe you will find the act both entertaining and of the most interest."

I was taken aback by Holmes's coyness, but I could see he wanted me to show patience. I simply nodded in understanding and left the detective to gaze upon the happiness he brought to our loyal street urchins. Before long, the Wild West show began. It was just as marvellous as the news reported, perhaps even more so.

Cody came charging out in the centre of the stage, riding Old Charlie, the famous 21 year old horse noted as Cody's favourite, who seemed to enjoy the attention as much as his human companion. "Ladies and Gentlemen," Mr Cody grandly called with a wave of his hat and a bow, "this evening you are in for a feast of the eyes as you journey thousands of miles across the sea and over the lands, past the Florida swamps and the Adirondack Mountains, to land in the true heart of America, that of the Wild West. Tonight, my friends, you will marvel at the sharp shooting of Annie

Oakley, spy an Indian attack on a pioneer stage coach, gasp at the acrobatic feats of Buck Taylor, and witness man conquer nature as a recreated wildfire appears before your very eyes. But enough talking from me, on with the show!"

A huge roar of approval and applause thundered from the audience as a herd of Buffalo rumbled onto the fairgrounds. Both cowboys and Indians worked together to corral the beasts and show a simulated hunt of the now almost extinct symbol of America. This act was followed by the great Annie Oakley. The sharpshooter known as "Little Sure Shot," threw two clay pigeons into the air. She then hurled herself toward a table where two rifles lay in wait. I expected the dame to pick up the nearest Winchester and shatter one of the fake birds. To my astonishment, the lady leaped over the table, grabbing both rifles and let off two shots even before her feet hit the ground. The pigeons shattered in the air, and the crowd went wild. Holmes was applauding and laughing, but I could see his eyes were on the raucous Irregulars.

After the great Annie Oakley came the stagecoach robbery. The wild Indians, adorned with war paint, whooping and hollering, riding horses bareback, launched a full attack on the circled wagons. The coachmen tried their best but were no match from the overwhelming onslaught of Indian arrows. The actors did a magnificent job falling over, pretending to be dead, and, for added effect, with an arrow emerging from their backs. Just as all seemed lost, a trumpet call came from off stage and the cavalry, led by Buffalo Bill himself, came charging out and drove the Red men away.

Again the audience seemed to lose their sense of decorum as they called, hollered, and cheered in a way to rival the whoops of the defeated Sioux. Next up came the cowboys. Buck Taylor and his compatriots held races, rode bucking broncos, re-enacted daily voyages of the Pony Express, leaped over fallen coaches, and picked up sombreros from the ground while their horses continued at full gallop. Mr Cody joined the group, riding his faithful companion. He had audience members toss baseballs into the air which he shot from the sky with his Colt army revolver, never slowing Old Charlie who continuously raced around the grounds at a furious pace.

Next came the astounding acrobats of John "the Ranger" Billings. "Ladies and Gentlemen," Cody dramatically started, "you will now witness mankind fighting that most monstrous beast of nature, that terrifying creature which consumes whole towns in its jaws, that horror known as the wildfire." The stage was set at a logging camp in the Rocky Mountains. A ranger station was on one side of the stage and on the other was a tower adorned with a bell to ring at any sign of danger. Two show hands set a pile of brush in the centre of the stage and set it ablaze. Suddenly, Mr Billings, in full ranger gear, burst out of the ranger station. He attempted to get to the bell tower, but the flames blocked his path. He showed concern with his flailing arms and tried several different pathways around the flames but to no avail.

The audience was absolutely silent, and I began to worry that perhaps the act had gotten out of hand, that the fire had shown a life of its own and perhaps we would be evacuating the building. I looked at the faces of the children in front of me and even scanned the audience to find most faces showing at the very least concern, if not absolute fright.

Just as I was about to suggest to Holmes we move towards the exits to help disperse the crowd, I witnessed the most staggering gymnastic skills my eyes had ever seen. The Ranger grabbed a long, thin yet sturdy, piece of lumber. A cry came up from the audience as Mr Billings then sprinted straight for the flames in the center of the stage. I felt my heart pounding, *What,* I wondered, *was this fool doing? Would he commit suicide before thousands?*

Then, the miracle occurred. Just as Mr Billings was about to reach the flames, he jabbed the pole into the ground and used the stick to vault himself over the wildfire and land at the top of the bell tower. The sound of the bell ringing was drowned out by the raucous roars from the audience. We were all on our feet, hooting and hollering, screaming for more, and we did not stop our applause even as the fire brigade entered the stage and extinguished the flames.

Our cheers must have sounded for a good ten minutes when, suddenly, what I witnessed, truly witnessed, dawned upon me. "Holmes!" I shouted. "The killer!"

*

It was about two in the afternoon that following day when an elegant landau arrived in front of 221 Baker Street and both Mr Cody and Mr Billings arrived at our doorstep. We warmly greeted the entertainers who made a contrasting pair. Cody with his long hair and whiskers, Billings with his shaved face and closely cropped hair.

"Do you really think you've got the varmint behind this fiasco?" Cody asked. Before Holmes could respond, a wagon pulled to the curb behind where Mr Cody's landau had just departed, and out stepped Lestrade, and three of his constables. There was a fourth man the group assisted in removing from the carriage who had a lame foot and a crutch. The men helped their crippled companion through the front door, and we heard them struggling up the stairs.

"We should help that young man," said Billings.

"Actually, I have a rather unusual request for you," said Holmes and he opened the door to his bedroom. "Please stay here, gentlemen, and await my call to come out. You will hear the conversation I am about to have with the officers of the law, but I ask that you remain silent and do not reveal the fact that you are here until told to do so. As you know Mr Cody, I can be trusted."

"If that's what you'd like Mr Holmes, well, okay then." Cody assented, and the two men entered the bedroom after which Holmes closed the door behind them.

Shortly thereafter, the constables finally reached the door to our sitting room. Holmes warmly welcomed them in and offered a couch for the lame officer to lay upon. After they entered, I noted that Holmes closed and locked the door behind them.

Rousseau was one of the constables present. The other two affable men were introduced as Constables Holly and Tiller, both young officers whose forms didn't quite fill out their uniforms giving them an unintended comic charm. The lame officer on the couch was introduced as Constable Fowler, a man closer to my own age with coal black hair and a crooked nose.

"Really, Holmes," Lestrade complained, "I don't know why you couldn't have gone to Constable Fowler's residence. Forcing him to climb those stairs is beyond my reasoning."

"As I find is almost always the case," Holmes muttered, but Lestrade did not respond either because he ignored my friend or did not hear him.

"Constable Fowler, like Rousseau, was an officer at the scene of the crime Friday evening. Watson, if you recall, he is the officer that Rousseau informed us had sprained his foot that night. I believe that Fowler witnessed the murderer as he fled from Old Montague Street."

Fowler shook his head. "Mr Holmes," he replied, "if I can help in anyway, I will. It was the dead of night, and I did not see anyone flee from the crime scene. I only arrived quickly because I reside on Old Montague myself. There were quite a few people running about, but I can't say I saw someone fleeing from the area."

"Fowler, please look over these photographs of members of Mr Cody's troop. I believe there is someone you will recognize," Holmes insisted and handed a pile of promotional photographs from Cody's show to the officer.

The constable took the photographs from Holmes and began looking them over. The collection was a menagerie of men, both Red and White. With each turn of the pictures came a shake of the head from Fowler. Finally, he reached the end of the pile and held aloft one picture of a bald strongman. "Possibly him, although he would have had a wig on, but there's something familiar about him."

Holmes looked crestfallen. "That man is Melvin Brady, a former member of Mr Cody's troop, who never made the

THE CASE OF THE VANISHED KILLER

voyage to London. I did not mean to include his picture in the mix. Ah," Holmes perked up. "There is one more photograph." He removed a small, folded paper from his pocket and handed it to the injured man.

Fowler looked at the photo and his eyes bulged from his face. With a swift motion the invalid was on his feet and dashing towards the door. He grabbed at the handle, attempting to turn it, and finding it locked.

Realizing his situation, the fiend turned towards Holmes. Wild eyed, teeth clenched like a wounded animal, he sprang at Holmes with an inhuman growl. He made it but three steps before Rousseau, Lestrade, and the other constables had grabbed him and thrown him to the floor.

"Holmes, what on earth is going on?" asked Lestrade, after the officers had restrained Fowler with some rope.

"Cody, Billings please come out now," Holmes called. "I believe you will recognize Mr Wendell Finke, a former employee of the Wild West show."

Lestrade was stunned to see the two showmen step out of Holmes's private room, and I noted a slight reddening of his features, tightening of his jaw, and clenching of his fists. "Really Holmes!" Lestrade growled. "Did we need these theatrics?"

Holmes did not answer the Inspector's question. He waited as both Cody and Billings looked over the still struggling form of Finke. I saw a slight recognition in Wild Bill's face, but Billings clearly knew the man before him. "Finke," Billings gasped. "What have you done to yourself?"

"Only what needed to be done to give what those two had coming to them!" spat Finke.

"Mr Finke was a member of Mr Cody's Wild West show," Holmes explained to Lestrade and the other officers. He handed them the last photograph he had shown to Finke which revealed the man in full cowboy regalia, but with blonde hair and a straight nose. "He was the assistant to Mr Billings and a noted acrobat. After the troop arrived in London in the spring, Mr Finke was part of the show until the end of April when he abruptly quit."

"That's right," Finke blurted, then held his tongue. The man was fuming, and we were not sure whether he would speak more, yell at us, or struggle against his bindings, or perhaps do all three at once.

Finally, with a heavy sigh, Finke seemed to decide that since he was caught anyway, he should tell his tale and explain his actions. "I had finally tracked down those Smith crooks. I had stumbled upon them in London. They had taken everything from me, the devils. I met them in New York, at my mother's funeral, though they weren't called Smith then. Then it was Roger and Mary Corbin. Roger claimed to be a stockbroker, claimed he could double my inheritance by investing in a horseless carriage company. I fell for it. I was the rube, I was. They took everything and fled. That was ten years ago almost to the day.

"Finding myself destitute, I sought out work, jobs that allowed me to move around as I tried to track down the Corbins. I almost caught up to them once in Chicago, but they disappeared again before I could find them. They always left rich men poor in their wake. Roger was a gambling man of the worst kind, the kind that does not know when to stop and always loses.

"Finally, in the fall, I joined Mr Cody's troop. I had given up on tracking down the Corbins. Their trail had gone stale, and I had moved on. Then, as fortune would have it, one day I was exploring London and ended up in a tavern on Old Montague. Who should I see making a wager with the barkeep? Why, Mr Roger Corbin. I saw him, but he did not recognize me. I followed the man, found out where he lived, who he was, that he hadn't stopped his wicked ways."

"That's when you decided to murder them?" Lestrade demanded.

"No. It had been years since I had seen them. I tried to put them out of my head. Tried my best, but I couldn't stop thinking about what they'd done, how they were still swindling people. After a few weeks, I decided to seek my revenge. I quit Mr Cody's show and became a constable. It was easy enough. There's quite a shortage of us," he motioned to the other officers present. "Anyway, I took lodging in the building next to the Corbins, now Smiths. I dyed my blonde hair black, and even got my nose smashed in a proper tavern brawl. I needed to make sure the couple wouldn't recognize me. As an officer, I occasionally, entered their tenement building. I noted how tight the hallways were, how crammed the stairwells. If I were to kill the couple, I most surely would be seen fleeing, especially if I was wearing my police outfit."

"But," Holmes interrupted, "you were an acrobat, a skilled knife thrower, and a man who knows how to walk a tight rope, or vault across a pit of fire. You will recall Watson that after inspecting the home of the Smiths, we wandered up to the building's roof and I noted a scuff mark in the in the roofing overlooking the Northeast side of the building. My first thought was that someone had laid a pole or thin ladder across the two buildings and that there were even possibly two assailants, one to hold the pole while the other scurried across it. The person who scurried to the other building would have to be someone who was extremely athletic. From the bloody footprints I noted the man's gait and knew he had to be about 5 feet in height, the exact height of Mr Finke. I also deduced that the man who killed the Smiths was someone that they knew, most likely from America, as one of the photographs of the couple in front of The Statue of Liberty, was crumpled slightly and off to the side, as if the killer had stared long at the image before discarding it. I also knew that the man had to be Anglo. Otherwise, someone would have noted a man of a different race, especially a Lakota Sioux, approaching or fleeing the tenement building.

"Extraordinary, Mr Holmes," remarked Rousseau. "Still how did you find that Finke was our man?"

"Ahh, well after Watson and I left the Smiths, I went to the tenement on the Northeast side of the building. If the assailants had escaped via the rooftop, there was a good chance they would have been seen returning down the stairs to their lodgings. I inquired with the building supervisor about the building tenants. He mentioned Officer Fowler. It dawned on me that a constable would have the means of committing the murders, return down to the street level, and cover up his tracks. I knocked on the officer's door, pretending to be a reporter for *The Times*. I noted the man's features and when I visited Mr Cody's grounds I stumbled upon Mr Billings practicing his wildfire act. After seeing the

THE CASE OF THE VANISHED KILLER

pole vaulting, I realized one man could easily have committed the crime. I inquired with Mr Billings about current and former members of the Wild West show capable of completing the pole vault. When he showed me the picture of Mr Finke, gentlemen, the case was closed."

"But how on earth did Finke get a vaulting pole?" Lestrade inquired.

"The missing pole!" suddenly Billings called out in shock then turned to the bound Finke, "You stole it!"

"That's right," Finke snarled. "I returned to the showground as an officer of the law. I stole the pole and returned to my building, then the next day, I went to the roof of the Smith residence and stashed the pole, ready to finally enact justice."

"But the pole?" Lestrade puzzled. "How did you transport such a large pole?"

"I believe Mr Billings can answer your question," Holmes interjected.

"Yes," answered Billings. "The pole is an invention of my own. I found bamboo bends quite easily and can achieve greater heights than hard wood; however, it is still difficult to transport an eight foot piece of wood. I created a five piece version where the pieces screw together to make the pole, quite similar to the newer cue sticks."

"Then everything was set," continued Holmes. "Finke entered the building in his police uniform. The Smiths, seeing a constable at their door, invited him in. Finke then dispatched the Smiths, climbed to the roof, removed his shoes, tossed them into the alley below, vaulted over to his own building, and then descended the stairs to his room where he put on new shoes. The accoster quickly went to the alley where he gathered the bloody shoes and the stick, which he disassembled, hid them in a bag or beneath his uniform, and then stashed them away in his own apartment. I would not be surprised, constables, if you were to find the materials still inside Finke's residence."

Lestrade looked stunned at all that had been revealed before him. "I assure you Mr Holmes, that my men will search his room after we bring him back to the Yard."

"Before you take Mr Finke away, I do have one question for him. Why did you set up Mr Cody's Lakota-Sioux?"

"I know those men, barbarians they are," grumbled Finke. "I figured there wasn't nothing I did to the Smiths that those warriors hadn't done a thousand times over to settlers. If an Indian hanged for the crime, so be it. There's a saying in America, that the only good Injun is a dead Injun."

Holmes's face was filled with absolute revulsion at Mr Finke. "I believe in your country, just as ours, all people are created equal, and all people are equal in the eyes of the law. You chose to take the law into your own hands. You committed a crime and now must face the punishment."

Finke lashed out with harsh words at my companion, words I cannot repeat in the confines of this narrative. My dear friend just stood quietly as the constables hauled away the murderer.

"I'm glad that's over," I said to my companion as the wagon took Finke away.

"I agree Watson. Finke believed he was serving a perverse form of justice. In the end he was actually a worse criminal than that of the Smiths. I believe he will learn true justice when he hangs from the end of a rope. And now, Watson, onto another puzzling dilemma," my friend stated.

"I hope it is not another grisly murder," I stated in astonishment.

No, no, I was deciding whether I should order the Quail or the Flounder at Simpson's this evening."

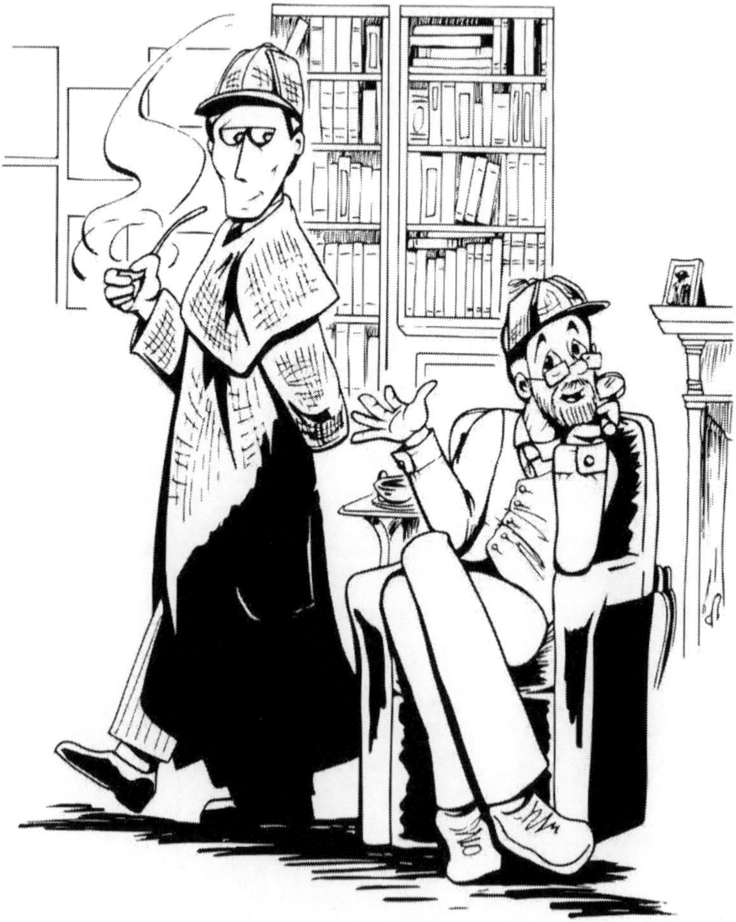

Author Interview with Derrick Belanger

DERRICK BELANGER

Q: Congratulations on your new publishing company. Do tell us more about it. Would you be doing only specific Sherlockian categories?

Thank you. My brother, Brian Belanger, and I decided this summer to give it a go and start our own publishing company, Belanger Books. What we've discovered is that there is a rich variety of excellent literature out there that just needs a publishing home. Currently we are focusing on children's literature, Golden Age science fiction and Steampunk, and, of course, Sherlock Holmes novels and stories. We are open to all literature that is of a high quality and is fairly family friendly. Having stated that, we do have the occasional book that would probably get an "R" rating such as the horror anthology *My Peculiar Family* which will have a Kickstarter campaign in January with a formal release in May. That one will be one of our first big books because it has some New York Times bestsellers in it like Tracy Hickman and Christopher Golden.

As far as Sherlock Holmes is concerned, we will have several Sherlock Holmes books come out next year, and we already have released the third MacDougall Twins with Sherlock Holmes book, *Curse of the Deadly Dinosaur*. I would like to say that Belanger Books was not created to be exclusively a Sherlock Holmes publisher. Watson didn't leave enough material behind for that to happen! But of course, I'm a Sherlockian and my brother is a Sherlockian, and pretty much every author who is working with us is a Sherlockian, so we will have a line of Sherlock Holmes titles.

AUTHOR INTERVIEW

We currently have three Holmes anthologies lined up for next year, plus an incredible Sherlock Holmes children's book entitled *Scones and Bones on Baker Street, Sherlock's Dog (Maybe) and the Dirt Dilemma* by Brenda Seabrooke. The novel is pure magic and should be a big hit with kids. There may be a few more Sherlockian titles depending on what is submitted to us and what we accept. If you've discovered an unwritten tale that Dr Watson left behind, and you decide to edit it, please send it our way. We love publishing new Sherlock Holmes stories.

Also, if someone out there has a book and is looking for a publisher, send us an inquiry at submissions@belangerbooks.com. We will definitely give you a read and let you know why we accept or reject your manuscript. I suppose that's the toughest part of publishing, having to tell an author that their book doesn't quite fit or doesn't meet our quality standards. But on the other side, it is a thrill to tell someone that we have accepted their book and will publish it.

Q: YOU ARE GENERALLY ON THE OTHER SIDE OF SHERLOCKIAN INTERVIEWS. IS IT VERY DIFFERENT?

This is a huge difference. Now I know how my interviewees feel. But this is also a lot of fun. I originally started doing author interviews on my blog because I thought it would be nice to go beyond reviewing books and actually give authors a chance to talk about their writing. My first author interview was with Kieran Lyne about his novel *The*

Last Confession of Sherlock Holmes, and then I followed that one with an interview with Geri Schear for her novel *A Biased Judgement: The Sherlock Holmes Diaries 1897*. Talk about starting off with a bang! Both those novels were in my top ten pastiches for 2014, and both of them were considered highly controversial. I won't go into the reasons why here. Let me just say that I am a bit of a purist when it comes to Holmes. I have to honour the original words of Dr Watson, and some books clearly go to other sources in telling their tales, but I do appreciate good writing. These two books were so well written that I could accept their controversial aspects. I followed with interviews with the great David Marcum, Daniel D. Victor, and Dan Andriacco.

Then in the spring of 2015, I was asked by Scott Monty to write for the blog *I Hear of Sherlock Everywhere*. That has been a wonderful experience because their blog has a much wider readership than my Goodreads blog. Instead of having a few hundred people reading my articles, I now have a few thousand. This has been wonderful because I've gotten to interview new Sherlock Holmes authors such as Kim Krisco and Gregg Rosenquist and bring their books to an audience of likely customers who may not have known their books existed.

I've also enjoyed interviewing many of the authors who participated with the MX Book of New Sherlock Holmes Stories and doing my small part to help save Undershaw, Doyle's former estate which has fallen into disrepair. Hopefully, the funds raised will allow Stepping Stones, a school for special needs students, to restore the estate to its former glory.

And I might add I'm most proud of the interview I did with Mitch Cullin, the author of *A Slight Trick of the Mind*, the novel which was the basis for the film, *Mr Holmes*. It is an outstanding piece on his dealings with the Doyle estate. Sadly, it had to be edited down some by his lawyers, but it is still a powerful piece about the importance of fighting to keep Sherlock free.

Q: You have been a Sherlockian for a long, long time. How did it happen?

I had enjoyed Sherlock Holmes stories growing up, but the first one to really grab me was, fittingly, *A Study in Scarlet*, when I was 14 years old. I chose the book out of a list of choices for an 8th grade mystery unit I was completing in my Language Arts class.

When I started reading the book, for the first half, I was immersed in Doyle's, or perhaps I should say Watson's, London, a London as equally magical and breath-taking as that of Dickens. I got introduced to most of the major characters in the canon, and enjoyed the gruesome murder mystery, a story of bloody revenge.

Then suddenly, as the story builds to a climax, the audience runs into a brick wall as the narrative suddenly shifts to the American West in 1847. I had never read a book which was split in two halves that appeared to be two completely different stories. Then, in a brilliant move, the author brings the two stories together in a masterful weaving of plot. I thought Doyle had such faith in his readers, to throw us such a jarring twist and expect us to keep reading to the end. Of course I did, and began gobbling up all of his Holmes stories.

Now before I move onto the next question, I should add that I was hooked on Watson and Doyle's Sherlock Holmes stories after reading *A Study in Scarlet*; however, I became hooked on Doyle's writings beyond those he shared with Watson a few years later. I was reading a random anthology of literature, the type where the stories are seemingly assembled because of who wrote them, not because of any cohesive theme. Smack in the middle of Shirley Jackson's "Charles," and Richard Connell's "The Most Dangerous Game," was Sir Arthur Conan Doyle's "The Horror of the Heights." When I read this story, I was stunned at the creativity of the writing, the imagination of the aerial world of beasts living above our heads. I didn't know Doyle beyond his contributions to the Sherlock Holmes stories. I was blown away and sought out any and all of his horror writings. This, in many ways, led to my two volume anthology, *A Study in Terror: Sir Arthur Conan Doyle's Revolutionary Stories of Fear and the Supernatural*. I wanted others, especially Sherlockians, to know Doyle's other stories and to see that some equalled his Holmes stories in literary merit and scholarly importance.

Q: TELL US ABOUT THE FAMOUS TWINS — AND THE NEWEST BOOK.

The MacDougall Twins with Sherlock Holmes is my series of books that focus on the MacDougall Twins, ten-year-old twin detectives who live at 222 Baker Street, across the street from Sherlock, and they work with the great detective on solving cases. The series came into existence because my oldest daughter, who was eight at the time, asked me, "Daddy, who is Sherlock Holmes?" I told her about the character and as the conversation continued we both thought it would be great if there was a child detective working with Sherlock Holmes. Eventually that idea developed into the MacDougall Twins with Sherlock Holmes series. The point of the books, specifically, is to introduce children to the Sherlock Holmes characters so that as they get older they will want to seek out the original stories in the canon. Now, I should add that I say this is my series, but really it is equally my brother's series. Brian illustrates the books, and while I think my stories are good, it is most definitely Brian's artwork which brings the twins to life.

It should be noted that even though this is a Sherlock Holmes series, the stars of the books are definitely the twins. We wanted kids to feel empowered by the books and to know that they are often just as intelligent as adults. They also have a different perspective than the adult characters which is very important in solving crimes. This is why Holmes, in the original canon, employed the Baker Street Irregulars.

Each book in the series gets a little more complex. The first book, *The Amazing Airship Adventure*, is designed for a third grade level reader. It is short and angled for fans of The Rainbow Fairy series or The Magic Treehouse books. The second book, *Attack of the Violet Vampire*, and the third book, *Curse of the Deadly Dinosaur*, are a little more complicated, but they are still aimed at primary school readers. Of course, there are in-jokes that fans of the canon will enjoy. My hope is that as the readers of this series age, they will read the original canon, then go back to the MacDougall Twins with Sherlock Holmes books and catch some of the jokes and connections with the original canon. For example, in *Attack of the Violet Vampire* there is a character named Bruce Partington. In *Curse of the Deadly Dinosaur*, the MacDougalls go undercover as the Baring-Goulds. There are a ton more canonical references, but I don't want to give them all away here.

The third book in the series, *Curse of the Deadly Dinosaur*, has the twins with Sherlock Holmes helping to solve the mystery behind a supposed prehistoric creature spotted in the hills of Surrey. Here's the description from the back cover:

Terror Strikes! During the Christmas season, a young man named Jonas Bogswell brings a most baffling case to Sherlock Holmes and the MacDougall Twins. A dinosaur with razor-sharp claws and a terrifying scream has been spotted roaming the hills of Surrey. But how can a prehistoric creature be alive in Victorian England? Police suspect Jonas Bogswell is really behind the attacks, and he needs the help of Sherlock Holmes, the MacDougall Twins and their faithful canine friend Toby to prove his innocence. Is Jonas completely innocent, or do he and his family have more knowledge of the dinosaur than they've revealed? Find out as the MacDougall Twins and Sherlock Holmes solve their most extraordinary case --- the Curse of the Deadly Dinosaur!

The series has gotten great reviews. Roger Johnson of the Sherlock Holmes Society of London called the books "…great fun…" and David Marcum said the third book in the series is "the best one yet!" We've also gotten wonderful feedback from students and teachers. Look for even more MacDougall Twins adventures in the future.

Q: What should Sherlockians expect from Belanger Books?

They can expect high quality pastiches. Some will be traditional, and some will be aimed for kids. They will all be respectful of the great detective. We will not publish stories where Holmes kills Watson, or Mycroft has an affair with Mary Watson, or the Great Hiatus was all a dream. While I think we will allow for some alternative universe publications with Holmes, they must keep Holmes essentially as Holmes. Currently we have three anthologies lined up which will be perfect reads for all Holmes fans.

The first book is called *Beyond Watson*. The idea for the book is that the authors have to tell the story from someone's perspective besides Dr John H. Watson. Watson can be in the story, and he may tell part of the story, but there has to be at least some of the story which goes beyond Watson's viewpoint. There are so many rich characters in the canon besides Watson that I thought it would be fun to have stories told from their points of view. David Marcum has submitted an excellent story told in part by Colonel Sebastian Moran. Marcia Wilson has a wonderful, dark tale told by Inspector Lestrade. Geri Schear has Mrs Hudson tell of how she met Sherlock Holmes. And that's just scratching the surface. There are excellent tales from Daniel D. Victor, Elizabeth Varadan, and even Nebula award winning author Jack McDevitt who wrote his first Sherlock Holmes story for the collection. We plan on running an Indiegogo campaign for the book in March, 2016 and publishing the anthology sometime in the summer. I know I'm biased, but I believe this book will be remembered as the best Sherlock Holmes book of 2016.

The other two Holmes anthologies are still accepting submissions. The first is *Before Watson: Sherlock Holmes in Montague Street*. The anthology is made up of stories which occurred before Holmes moved to Baker Street and before he met Watson. The other anthology is called *Holmes Away from Home: Tales of the Great Hiatus*. That anthology is made up of stories that occur from May 4th, 1891 – April 5th, 1894, when the world believed that Sherlock Holmes had perished over the Reichenbach Falls. That anthology will have some Holmes stories, but I am also looking for stories that deal with other characters from the canon living in a world without Holmes. I have a few story submissions for both anthologies, but I am looking for more, ten total. If someone out there reading this interview would like to submit a story for either *Before Watson* or *Holmes Away from Home*, please submit your story with an author bio to Belanger Books at submissions@belangerbooks.com. Stories should be between 5,000 – 10,000 words in length, though you can go over or under some. Honestly, if the story is great, we'll publish it! Just make sure to get your anthology entry in by June 1, 2016.

In addition to the anthologies we have the excellent children's book *Scones and Bones on Baker Street, Sherlock's Dog (Maybe) and the Dirt Dilemma* by Brenda Seabrooke. The book is a unique retelling of "The Red Headed League,"

AUTHOR INTERVIEW

but it is told from the perspective of Digby, a homeless dog trying to be adopted by Sherlock Holmes. Like The MacDougall Twins books, this one will be an excellent way for children to get to know the character of Sherlock Holmes and grow up with him.

And who knows what else will be submitted to Belanger Books? If there is a well written Sherlock Holmes book someone would like to submit to Belanger Books, please send it to submissions@belangerbooks.com. We guarantee we will read it and let you know what we think.

Q: YOU HAVE A NEW NOVELLA OUT FROM ENDEAVOUR PRESS CALLED *SHERLOCK HOLMES: THE ADVENTURE OF THE PECULIAR PROVENANCE*. TELL US A LITTLE BIT ABOUT THIS BOOK. ALSO, WHY ISN'T THIS BOOK A BELANGER BOOKS RELEASE?

That's a great question with a bit of an interesting answer. As I explain in the introduction to this book, the tin box that contained the letters between Dr Watson and his nephew, Archibald Adams, was presented to me by the mother of two children that I tutor. The box contains letters from a correspondence between Watson and Adams which went on for many decades. *The Adventure of the Peculiar Provenance* is the first book I have compiled from their letters. It was quite a task to put together a story based on letters written in two different styles of English, one British and one American.

Once I finished the story, I submitted the novella to Endeavour Press in June of 2015, just before I'd made the decision to start Belanger Books. Originally, I thought I'd include the piece in *The MX Book of New Sherlock Holmes Stories*. As I compiled the story, I got to 12,000 words and knew there was no way I could make this fit into a short story collection. So, I put Peculiar Provenance on the side, wrote the story "The Case of the Vanished Killer" for the anthology, which was a much shorter piece from the Watson letters, and then I returned to *Peculiar Provenance* and found the story to be over 25,000 words. Knowing this would be too short for a paperback book, I searched online and found that Endeavour Press had a line of Sherlock Holmes ebooks. I submitted the manuscript to them, and voila, it was accepted and published on November 1, 2015. The ebook has gotten very good early reviews, and it has sold well. Plus, Endeavour has been kind enough to allow Belanger Books to publish the paperback version of the novella which you now hold in your hands.

I think the back cover description of the novella explains the story perfectly, so there's no need to retell it here. I will state that the tale also has quite a bit of action and espionage, and many people have told me it is a page turner. Even nearly 100 years after his death, Watson's writing still captivates readers.

Due to the ebook's success, I am planning a series of Sherlock Holmes books with Endeavour where they will publish the ebook and Belanger Books will publish the softcover edition. Next up is *Sherlock Holmes and the Adventure of the Primal Man* where Holmes is hired by a member of the British Museum to determine the authenticity

AUTHOR INTERVIEW

of a supposed Yeti body brought to London from Mt. Everest. I hope it is just as successful as *Peculiar Provenance*.

I would also like to add that just because I've started my own publishing company doesn't mean that I won't work with other publishers. In fact, I am submitting stories to both Volumes 4 and 5 of *The MX Book of New Sherlock Holmes Stories*. I could never turn down an opportunity to write Holmes stories for such wonderful books.

Q: WHAT HAS SURPRISED YOU ABOUT THE NEW WATSON WRITINGS YOU'VE DISCOVERED?

The first surprise is just how many unwritten stories there are out there. I think Watson had two full time jobs. He was a doctor and a writer, but I think he spent more time with his pen than he did with his patients. Second, specifically referring the letters I have been reading from the correspondence between Watson and Adams, I have been surprised at how informal the language comes across sometimes. Holmes referred to Mrs Watson as Mary, at least according to Watson's letters. It could simply be that since these are letters, Watson took a less formal tone. This is also true of the language in some of Sir Arthur Conan Doyle's letters.

Q: MAY I PUT UP YOUR STANDARD QUESTION BACK AT YOU? IF YOU WERE STRANDED ON AN UNINHABITED ISLAND WITH ONLY ONE SHERLOCKIAN TALE FOR COMPANY, WHICH ONE WOULD YOU CHOOSE?

That's been called the meanest question to ask a Sherlockian. My feeling is that depending on the day, my answer might change. Watson was such an exceptional writer, and all the stories have his unique flare in them. My gut reaction is to always name "The Man with the Twisted Lip." The story has that great way of starting with one narrative thread and then shifting into a completely different story. It also shows the sinister underbelly of London with Watson's descent into the opium den searching for Isa Whitney, and it shows how one can work around the British class system, making a handsome salary as a beggar. To top it all off, you also have Mary Watson calling her husband James instead of John, a great puzzle we Sherlockians love to try to solve. I could also name "The Speckled Band" because it is such a rich gothic horror story with a wonderful surprise ending. From what I understand it is also the first story with the death clue, where a character says a clue about the murder just before dying. The detective has to figure out what the death clue means. In this case we have Julia Stoner saying she was killed by the Speckled Band. What is the Speckled Band? It's up to Holmes to solve the mystery. Still, I think I'll stick with "The Man with the Twisted Lip" for now. Maybe tomorrow, I'll choose "The Musgrave Ritual."

Q: SOME STANDARD QUESTIONS — FAVOURITE PASTICHE AND FAVOURITE MEDIA ADAPTATIONS, AND THE REASONS FOR YOUR CHOICE.

Favourite pastiche should be even more difficult than favourite tale from the canon. There are so many incredible

AUTHOR INTERVIEW

pastiche stories out there now, literally thousands. But in the end, I wouldn't even hesitate for a second to name my favourite, and that would have to be *Sherlock Holmes of Baker Street* by William S. Baring–Gould. I rank that book as second place to the original canon in its importance, and the book is a fun read. It is a full biography of the life of Sherlock Holmes, and it incorporates some of the original stories into its narrative. Of course, in many ways, this book is just as controversial as more recent books because it has Holmes and Irene Adler having a relationship resulting in the birth of Rex Stout. It also has some alternative universe material in that Holmes and Watson have to chase down Professor Challenger's missing pterodactyl which got loose in London at the end of *The Lost World*. Even with those segments, the book is wonderfully clever, and it helps bring Holmes and Watson to life. We also get a timeline in the back of the book which explains when Watson was married to his first wife, Constance Adams, and it tells of the death of Holmes at the ripe old age of 103 on January 6th, 1957. I don't think anything close to the importance of *Sherlock Holmes of Baker Street* was published until Leslie S. Klinger completed his annotated editions of the canon in 2005.

Favourite media adaptation is also very easy. Hands down, it has to be the Granada series. I grew up with Jeremy Brett as Sherlock Holmes. He is Sherlock Holmes to me. I hear his voice when I write Holmes. I picture Edward Hardwicke by his side as Watson. Every year, I go back and watch a few episodes of the series. I could keep my eyes closed the whole time and just listen to their voices. God! That series! What an astounding achievement!

DERRICK BELANGER

Q: IF YOU HAD TO INTERVIEW SHERLOCK HOLMES AND JOHN WATSON, WHAT QUESTIONS WOULD YOU ASK THEM? WHY?

First, I doubt very much Holmes would allow me into his sitting room. If he found out I was writing stories about him, and I didn't have the relationship which he has with Watson, I'd be shown the door. But, pretending for the moment, that he did see me, I would ask the gentlemen about their friendship. The crux of the Holmes stories is the dear friendship between the two men. It is, in my opinion, the strongest example of a masculine friendship told in literature. How did that friendship survive all those years? How were the two men able to forgive each other, especially when the other's behaviour got on one's nerves?

I suppose I'd also ask some of the standard questions about cases and the like, but I'd really just want to get to know the gentlemen. Maybe have a few drinks along the way.

Q: WHAT DO YOU THINK OF THE CURRENT SHERLOCK HYPE?

By current Sherlock hype, I am assuming that you are referring to all the new incarnations of Sherlock Holmes and not just the show *Sherlock*. We are living in a Sherlockian renaissance at the moment. While I credit the show *Sherlock* for being the frontrunner of that trend, I love all the current incarnations of Sherlock Holmes including Elementary, the Robert Downey Jr. Sherlock Holmes films, the Russian television show, and all the incredible pastiches which are being written and published, thanks in large part to MX publishing.

I know some purists really don't like the more modern takes on Sherlock Holmes, and I admit there are times when I've been so upset about a change in how a character acts on one of the new shows that I find myself throwing pillows at the television set. Even with that grumbling on my part, these shows have brought a new audience to the original stories. People talk about Sherlock Holmes much more now than they have ever during my lifetime. My students are excited about Sherlock Holmes. Sure they use the term mind palace instead of brain attic, but who cares? Okay. I know. Quite a few people care, but personally, I think mind palace is going to become part of the unofficial canon like the bent briar pipe and the saying "Elementary, my Dear Watson." My feeling is that the more people who come to Sherlock Holmes, the better.

Q: IF SHERLOCK HOLMES TURNED UP IN YOUR BACKYARD ONE EVENING, FULLY AWARE OF THE THINGS YOU DO FOR HIM, WHAT DO YOU THINK HE WOULD SAY TO YOU?

My gut reaction is to think he'd probably be upset with me. He wasn't thrilled that Watson was telling melodramatic versions of his stories, and now there is an army of writers retelling all of his cases. And I'm one soldier in that army. But I also think Holmes had a good sense of humour, and he might laugh the whole thing off. After all, he wanted his fame to rest on his *Whole Art of Detection* book. Maybe he'd see that we pastiche authors are tapping into what David Marcum likes to call The Great Watsonian Oversoul, and in many ways, we are writing his *Whole Art of Detection*. We are telling his untold tales. We are keeping his name alive. The readers of our stories today are the ones who will make the forensic breakthroughs tomorrow. For that, he might even give me a wink and say, "Good show."

Special Thanks

The author would like to thank all of the people who offered feedback and advice while he wrote this exceptional story: David Marcum, Gregg Rosenquist, Jay Ganguly, Kim Krisco, Chuck Davis, Brian Belanger. Without your valuable insights, he couldn't have made this delightful adventure.

The author would also like to thank Sir Arthur Conan Doyle for creating the world's greatest literary character; Dr Watson's Neglected Patients, his local Sherlock Holmes Scion Society; Scott Monty for the opportunity to write for *I Hear of Sherlock Everywhere*; Steve Emecz for being the first publisher to see his writing potential, his parents, Dennis and Ellen Belanger, and grandmother, Barbara Rousseau, for their support; his in-laws Marc and Deborah Gosselin (pretty much the entire Gosselin clan) for their support; Keith and Sherlene Searight, Luis Uribe and Darcie Matsunaga, and Barbara Sterling for their pledge and support during the BVUUF 2015 auction; Traci Belanger, for letting Brian out to play; Abigail Gosselin, his wife, and Rhea and Phoebe, his daughters for not minding too much the time the writing took away from family, play time, and chores; and to the entire Sherlockian community for keeping the spirit of Sherlock Holmes alive and well. May he always remain the man who never lived and so can never die.

About the Author

Derrick Belanger is an author and educator most noted for his books and lectures on Sherlock Holmes and Sir Arthur Conan Doyle. Both volumes of his two volume anthology *A Study in Terror*: *Sir Arthur Conan Doyle's Revolutionary Stories of Fear and the Supernatural* were #1 best sellers on the Amazon.com UK Sherlock Holmes book list, and his MacDougall Twins with Sherlock Holmes chapter book, *Attack of the Violet Vampire*! was also a #1 bestselling new release in the UK. Mr Belanger's academic work has been published in The Colorado Reading Journal and Gifted Child Today. Mr Belanger is also a teacher at Century Middle School in the Adams 12 Five Star School District, and he resides in Broomfield, Colorado with his wife, Abigail Gosselin, and their daughters, Rhea and Phoebe.